PUFF

MORRIS GLEITZMAN

Gift of the Gab

Morris Gleitzman was born and educated in England. He went to Australia with his family in 1969 and studied for a degree. In 1974 he began work with the ABC, left to become a full-time film and television writer in 1978 and has written numerous television scripts. He has two children and lives in Sydney, but visits England regularly. One of the best-selling children's authors in Australia, his first children's book was *The Other Facts of Life*, based on his award-winning screenplay. This was followed by the highly acclaimed *Two Weeks with the Queen,* and he has now written several other books for children including *Second Childhood* and most recently the *Wicked!* series with Paul Jennings.

Some other books by Morris Gleitzman

BUMFACE
TWO WEEKS WITH THE QUEEN
THE OTHER FACTS OF LIFE
SECOND CHILDHOOD

The WICKED! *series*

1: THE SLOBBERERS
2: BATTERING RAMS
3: CROAKED
4: DEAD RINGER
5:THE CREEPER
6: TILL DEATH US DO PART

MORRIS GLEITZMAN

GIFT OF
THE GAB

PUFFIN BOOKS

For my grandparents

PUFFIN BOOKS

Published by the Penguin Group
Penguin Books Ltd, 27 Wrights Lane, London W8 5TZ, England
Penguin Putnam Inc., 375 Hudson Street, New York,
New York 10014, USA
Penguin Books Australia Ltd, Ringwood, Victoria, Australia
Penguin Books Canada Ltd, 10 Alcorn Avenue, Toronto, Ontario,
Canada M4V 3B2
Penguin Books (NZ) Ltd, Private Bag 102902, NSMC, Auckland,
New Zealand

On the World Wide Web at: www.penguin.com

Penguin Books Ltd, Registered Offices: Harmondsworth,
Middlesex, England

First published in Australia in paperback by Penguin Books
Australia Ltd 1999
Published in Great Britain by Viking 1999
Published in Puffin Books 2000
1 3 5 7 9 10 8 6 4 2

Made and printed in England by Clays Ltd, St Ives plc

British Library Cataloguing in Publication Data
A CIP catalogue record for this book is available from the British Library

ISBN 0–140–38798–6

It's not fair.

I don't reckon the police should lock people up without hearing their side of the story.

My side of the story's really simple.

I did it, but there was a reason.

I tried to explain to Sergeant Cleary why I did it. In the police car I wrote down in my notebook everything that happened today. Even the things that'll probably make Dad send me to bed early when he hears about them.

I showed my statement to Sergeant Cleary while he was locking me in this cell.

'Not now, Rowena,' he said.

I could see he wasn't interested, though that might have been because Dermot Figgis was trying to bite him.

Police officers in small country towns have it really tough. The police stations are always understaffed. The only other officer on duty here today is Constable Pola, but he has to stay at the front desk in case of emergency calls or exciting developments in the car racing on TV.

Once Sergeant Cleary got Dermot into a cell, I tried to explain again. I banged on a wall pipe with my pen, like they do in prison movies.

'Message from Rowena Batts,' I banged in Morse code. 'I only did it because of the dog poo.'

That was ten minutes ago.

Sergeant Cleary hasn't been back.

He probably doesn't know Morse code. Either that or I didn't send it properly because my hands are shaking so much from outrage at Dermot Figgis and from worry about what's going to happen to me.

Sergeant Cleary's probably ringing Dad now.

'Mr Batts?' he's probably saying. 'We've got Rowena in the lock-up. We'll be charging her and putting her on trial as a criminal.'

Just thinking about it gives me a lump in the guts bigger than Antarctica.

Poor Dad. I hate putting him through this. The shame. And the lawyer's fees. He's got enough on his plate with the root weevil in the back paddock.

If only the police would listen to me.

That's the worst thing about being born with bits missing from your throat and not being able to talk with your voice, some people just won't listen to you.

2

Which means they never hear your side of the story.

The police are hearing Dermot Figgis's side. They can't help hearing it, he's been yelling it from the next cell for the last fifteen minutes.

'Rowena Batts attacked my car,' he's yelling. 'She filled it up with stewed apples.'

He's right, I did, but as I said before, there was a reason.

It's all here in my notebook. Including diagrams so the jury at my trial can see exactly what happened.

Some of the diagrams are bit wobbly. It's hard to do neat drawing while your hands are trembling with outrage and indignation. The dog-poo diagram for example. It looks more like two shrivelled sausages. I'd better label it so there's no misunderstanding.

And I'd better draw a diagram of the war memorial so the jury can see where the whole thing started.

This morning at the Anzac Day dawn ceremony.

Anzac Day's a very special day for me and Dad. It's our most important day of the year, including Christmas, birthdays and the release of a new Carla Tamworth CD.

It's the day Mum died.

So if anyone spoils it, I get pretty ropable.

I started getting ropable with Dermot Figgis at about 6.05 this morning.

As the first rays of the sun appeared over the supermarket, the crowd around the war memorial went quiet and Mr Shapiro played 'The Last Post' on his trumpet. Then we started the two-minute silence for the Aussie soldiers and other people who died in wars.

Dad reckons there were millions of them, including his grandfather who died in World War One, so even though it's not the most important part of the day for me, I try to concentrate.

This morning it was impossible.

Dermot Figgis and some of his hoon mates were doing the sausages. The footy club always does a sausage sizzle on Anzac Day so people who get emotionally drained by the ceremony can have a hot breakfast after.

As the two-minute silence began, Dermot started chopping onions really loudly.

Everyone glared at him, including me.

Then I glanced anxiously at old Mr Wetherby. He was actually in World War One and saw quite a few of his mates die. It can really stress you if you're trying to think about people who've died and other people are chopping onions noisily, specially if you're ninety-eight.

I could see Mr Wetherby trembling in his wheelchair. For a sec I thought he was so angry he was having a seizure. Then I realised he was just excited because he was being filmed by a TV crew as one of the oldest diggers in the state.

Dermot carried on chopping.

I decided if I go that selfish and dopey when I'm eighteen, I'll book myself in for a brain transplant.

I should have given Dermot a brain transplant there and then.

I would have done if I'd known what he was going to do half an hour later.

The two-minute silence ended and Dad stepped forward and cleared his throat.

Everyone stared. Some people looked cross and others rolled their eyes.

'Oh no,' someone muttered.

I couldn't believe it. What were they upset about? They all knew Dad was going to sing, he does every year.

It couldn't have been his clothes. Me and Dad got up extra early this morning and put a lot of effort into choosing him a respectful Anzac Day outfit. Black boots. Black jeans. Black shirt except for a tiny bit of yellow fringing. And he'd swapped his cow-skull belt buckle for one with an angel riding a really clean Harley.

The TV cameraman swung his camera away from Mr Wetherby and pointed it at Dad. I don't think he'd seen an apple farmer that well-dressed before.

Mr Cosgrove, the president of the Anzac Day committee, was glaring at Dad even harder than he'd been glaring at Dermot Figgis.

'Excuse me,' I said to Mr Cosgrove sternly. 'I think you're forgetting something. Anzac Day isn't just the day we remember the victims of war, it's also the day my mother died.'

Mr Cosgrove didn't understand all the words, of course, because he doesn't speak sign language, but I could tell he got the gist because he gave a big sigh.

Dad sang the song he always sings at the Anzac Day dawn ceremony. It's a beautiful Carla Tamworth country and western ballad about a truck driver whose wife dies and for the rest of his life he refuses to sell his truck because it's got the impression of her bottom in the passenger seat.

It makes me very sad, that song, because Mum died soon after I was born, so I haven't got those sorts of lasting memories of her.

It affected everyone else too, even though Dad's not that great a singer. Mr Wetherby dabbed away a tear and quite a few other people put their heads in their hands.

I could tell everyone was having strong feelings.

All except Dermot Figgis.

I heard giggling and turned and there was Dermot, dopey blond dreadlocks jiggling as he and his mates pointed at Dad and stuffed hot-dog buns in their mouths to stop themselves laughing.

They weren't doing a very good job.

World War One exploded in my head.

I stormed over to Dermot, determined to shut him up.

On the way I picked up a large plastic bottle of mustard.

The human brain's a weird thing.

When it's scared it stops working.

Mine did just now, when I heard Sergeant Cleary coming along the corridor towards the cells.

He's here to charge me, I thought, and transfer me to a remand centre for juvenile offenders.

Then my brain switched itself off.

I know why it did that. I spent five years in a special school once because of my throat problems and I never want to go back to an institution again. Not even if I end up a top surgeon or private detective. I won't charge kids from institutions who need treatment or a missing pet or parent found, but I won't be able to go to them, they'll have to come and see me on my yacht.

It's OK, but. Sergeant Cleary didn't charge me. Not yet. He just came down to tell Dermot Figgis to be quiet.

Dermot's brain went into hibernation too when he saw me storming towards him this morning holding a large bottle of mustard.

The whole town knows I stuffed a live frog into a kid's mouth once, a kid who wasn't respectful to Mum's memory, and Dermot must have thought I was planning to squeeze a bottleful of mustard into his.

I wasn't. I was just going to threaten him with it, that's all.

Dermot stepped away uncertainly, trod on a raw sausage, slipped, fell backwards and ended up sitting in a plastic bin full of ice and water and drink cans.

His mates cacked themselves.

Dermot's face went dark red.

That's when I did a dumb thing. I put my hand out to help him up.

When I think about it now, I feel faint. Dermot's years older than me and he could have crushed my hand like sausage meat in that big paw of his.

He didn't, but.

He let me pull him up. Then, as his mates went silent and embarrassed, he realised what he'd done and snatched his hand away.

He glared down at me with narrow eyes.

'You're history, kid,' he growled.

'Cheese-brain,' I replied. He doesn't speak sign, but I could tell he got the gist because his face went an even darker red.

Shaking, I went back over to Dad and concentrated on listening to the last few verses of the song.

When Dad finished, rather than let any more hoons spoil our sad mood further, we hopped onto the tractor and went over to the cemetery.

Or we would have done if the tractor hadn't broken down halfway there.

'Poop,' said Dad, using his mouth, which he always does when he's cross with himself.

I knew Dad was wishing we'd brought the truck. The only reason we brought the tractor was because it was hooked up to a trailer-load of mouldy apples Dad had promised Mr Lorenzini for his pigs.

It wasn't so bad. We had the tractor going in under an hour. It would have been less, but the apples attracted a lot of flies so we could only work one-handed.

The tractor broke down again halfway into the cemetery carpark.

'You go on ahead, Tonto,' said Dad. 'I'll fix this mongrel and catch you up.'

I was really pleased to hear him say that, partly because I really wanted to get to Mum's grave, and partly because I could tell he wasn't angry.

Tonto was a character in his favourite TV show when he was a kid, and he never calls me it when he's angry.

That's an example of why my dad's so special. A lot of dads, if the tractor was being a real mongrel, would get totally and completely ropable and spoil the most special day of the year.

Not my dad.

No, it's me who ended up doing that.

I knew there was something wrong with Mum's grave even before I got close to it.

It's in the top part of the cemetery with a really good view over the town. Because it's on a slope, you can see the flat grassy part of the grave as well as the headstone when you climb up to it.

I saw two small black things on the grassy part.

I knew they weren't lizards because they didn't scuttle off as I crunched towards them through the dry grass.

When I saw what they were, I felt a stab in the guts.

Dog poo.

Some mangy mongrel had done a poo on my most special place in the world.

Luckily, I always carry tissues on Anzac Day. I pulled a handful from my pocket, grabbed the two long hard shrivelled black objects and chucked them as hard as I could into the bush at the back of the graveyard.

'Sorry, Mum,' I whispered.

Then I heard Dad crunching towards me, so I stuffed the tissues back into my pocket.

He didn't have to know.

No point making him suffer too.

Funny, me thinking that. Given what's happened since. Dad wouldn't have suffered half as much from a bit of dog poo as he will when he finds out what I've done.

Oh well, at least we had our special time with Mum today.

'You OK, Tonto?' said Dad after we'd sat by the grave for about half an hour, alone with our feelings.

'I'm fine,' I replied. 'What about you?'

Dad's been a bit depressed lately. He always gets a bit depressed around Mum's anniversary. This year he's been more down than usual. I reckon it's the root weevil in the back paddock.

'I'm fine too,' said Dad. 'Now we've had our special time.'

That's the great thing about a dad who can speak with his hands. You can have a conversation even when both your throats are clogged up with tears.

We stood up and gave each other the hug Mum would have given us if she'd been around.

That's when I heard it.

A horrible, braying, jeering sound coming from the trees at the top of the cemetery.

Dermot Figgis and his hoon mates.

They swaggered out into the open, yelling and pointing to us and laughing.

I realised what the braying sound was.

Dermot was singing Mum's special song. The one Dad had sung at the war memorial. OK, Dermot could do the tune a bit better than Dad, but he was doing it in a mocking, sneering voice.

My guts knotted.

Then suddenly I knew.

The dog poo.

Suddenly I knew how it had got onto Mum's grave.

A dog didn't leave it there.

A mongrel did.

I stared at Dermot and World War One and World War Two both exploded in my head at the same time.

Dad put a hand on my arm.

'Ignore him,' he muttered. 'He'll get his.'

Dad was right about that.

A couple of lines into the song, Dermot forgot the words, which Dad would never do. Dermot gave us the finger and ran laughing into the trees with the other hoons.

I don't remember Dad leading me back to the carpark.

All I remember is what I saw there behind some bushes up the other end of the carpark from the tractor.

My heart started thumping so hard I thought my special black Anzac Day T-shirt was going to rip.

Dermot Figgis's car.

I knew it was his because he's the only person in town with a 1983 Falcon sprayed purple.

Dad hadn't seen it. He was too busy frowning at the tractor.

'I don't reckon she'll make it to Lorenzini's place hauling all these apples,' said Dad, unhooking the trailer. 'The distributor's gunna cark it any sec. How do you feel about staying here with the trailer while I go and ask Mr Lorenzini to come and fetch you and the apples?'

I found myself nodding really hard.

'If those hoons come back, just ignore 'em,' said Dad. 'They're all whistle and wind.'

I pretended not to hear him.

Dad gave me a squeeze and chugged off on the tractor.

As soon as he was out of sight, I dragged the trailer up to the other end of the carpark. It took ages and I nearly dislocated my shoulder, but I did it.

Then I grabbed the spade off the back of the trailer, opened Dermot's driver's door and started shovelling gunky apples into his car as fast as I could.

It was hot work, but I got them all in. When I'd finished, the cow-pattern seat covers were buried and you couldn't see much of the steering wheel.

Then I had an extra idea. I groped down into the squishy apples till I felt Dermot's keys in the ignition. I started the engine, groped some more till I found the heater knob, switched the heater on full and locked all the doors.

Revenge felt good.

But only for a sec.

Dermot's angry yell, ringing out across the carpark, put an end to that.

The human heart's almost as weird as the human brain.

It does exactly the same skip when you feel love as when you feel fear.

Mine did it just then, when I heard Sergeant Cleary coming back again with someone else. The other footsteps sounded like Dad. He's got metal tips on the heels of his cowboy boots and they click on lino.

The thought of seeing Dad made my heart skip with love.

The thought of him seeing me here in a cell made my heart skip with fear at exactly the same time.

Then, after all that, it wasn't Dad, it was Dermot's mum. She must have metal tips on her heels too.

When I saw her hair bobbing past the window in my cell door, my heart skipped again. It always does when I see people's mums. It's not love or fear, but. I think it might be jealousy.

My heart's been doing a lot of skipping today.

It did a huge one earlier when I saw Dermot and his mates running at me across the carpark, yelling furiously.

For a sec I stood, frozen.

I thought I could hear stewed apples bubbling away behind me in Dermot's car, but then I realised it was my tummy churning with fear.

My heart started pumping and I ran.

I thought I could get away because even though I'm much smaller than Dermot, I'm a good runner. Dermot and his mates play footy, but they also smoke and eat heaps of sausages.

Boy, was I wrong.

Dermot must have been doing extra training, or perhaps he was just extra furious, because I could hear his pounding feet getting closer behind me as I sprinted along the road back to town.

The road's called Memorial Drive. It's lined with trees and each tree's got a metal plaque on it in memory of a soldier who was killed in World War One. Their families planted the trees when that war ended, so the trees are over eighty years old and pretty big.

I was grateful for that today.

When I started hearing Dermot's angry breath behind me, wet and raspy, I knew my only chance was to be a better climber than him.

Dad's taught me a lot about climbing trees, including how you should never rush at one.

Except in emergencies.

I rushed at the nearest tree.

The trunk was big and smooth, but Dad once showed me some tricks for getting up big smooth trees. Luckily my hands weren't too sweaty and soon I was hauling myself up onto the first branch.

I clambered up into the high branches among the foliage.

Below I could hear Dermot swearing. I was in luck again. His mum didn't seem to have shown him any tree-climbing tricks.

My heart was skipping all over the place as I wrapped my arms round a branch and listened to the hoons trying to form a human pyramid. I could half-see them through the leaves. The pyramid kept collapsing and there was lots of swearing about people standing on other people's faces.

Then something ripped through the leaves close to my face.

And again.

'Aim for her head,' one of the hoons yelled.

They were chucking rocks at me.

I huddled against the branch, desperately hoping there were enough leaves to camouflage me. And wishing it was an apple tree so at least

I'd have something to chuck back at them.

More rocks crashed through the leaves.

I heard a car approaching. It slowed down, then drove on.

'That's illegal,' shouted one of the hoons at the car. 'Driving and using a mobile. I'm calling the cops.'

The driver must have beat him to it because about ten minutes later, just as I'd decided to climb down and offer to show the hoons how to throw straight in return for my freedom, I heard Sergeant Cleary's siren approaching.

'Run!' someone yelled.

'No,' shouted Dermot. 'I want the cops to see what she's done.'

Sergeant Cleary made the hoons stand on the other side of the road while I climbed down. As I slid down the trunk past the metal plaque I noticed the tree was in memory of Private Ern Wilson, killed 1917, aged nineteen.

'Thanks, Ern,' I said silently.

When Sergeant Cleary saw the apples cooking in Dermot's car, his mouth gave a little grin before he could stop it. The police in our town have had a lot of trouble with Dermot's car.

Dermot went mental.

'It's not funny,' he yelled and tried to grab me.

Sergeant Cleary pushed Dermot back. He wasn't smiling now.

'You're right, son,' he said. 'It's a serious crime, attempted assault. Do it again and I'll take you both in.'

Dermot tried to grab me again.

Sergeant Cleary took us both in.

Except that Dermot's being released now.

I can see him and his mum out in the corridor. She's got her arms round him in a big hug.

He's lucky, having a mum who's got a motel. Sergeant Cleary's got a lot of rellies who visit from interstate.

Why are my eyes going all hot and damp? Police perks are a fact of life, nothing to get upset about.

It's not that.

There's another reason my cheeks are wet.

Watching Mrs Figgis hug Dermot makes my heart give the most painful skip of all.

Because even if I sit in this cell for the rest of my life, my mum can never come here and hug me and set me free.

I still can't believe it.

There I was, mentally preparing myself for jail, feeling lucky I can have these conversations in my head so at least I wouldn't get too bored in the clink, not for the first couple of years at least, when suddenly I heard a rattling and Sergeant Cleary opened my cell door.

'OK,' he said, 'hop it.'

I stared at him.

'Off home,' he said, 'and don't upset any more eighteen-year-olds.'

'But,' I said, gobsmacked, 'aren't I under arrest?'

Sergeant Cleary watched my hands closely, frowning, but he didn't understand.

I wrote it in my notebook and showed him.

He gave a weary grin. 'No, Rowena,' he said. 'You're not under arrest. What you did was technically a crime, but under the circs, given that Dermot Figgis had it coming, and given the stress you must be under with that dopey dad of yours, I've decided not to charge you.'

As I followed Sergeant Cleary down the corridor to the front desk, I wrote indignantly in my notebook.

'What do you mean, dopey dad?'

Sergeant Cleary gave a sigh.

'I don't mean anything,' he said. 'I'm just saying it must be tough for you having a dad who's a bit of a ratbag.'

For a sec I couldn't speak. My hands were rigid with anger. I wondered how many years in jail I'd get for filling up a police car with rotting apples. We've got heaps more back at the orchard.

Constable Pola looked up from the TV.

'Don't get us wrong,' he said. 'Your old man's a nice bloke. It's just that he's a bit of a disaster area in the singing and clothing departments.'

It was an outrage. The police are meant to be tolerant and understanding. We did a project on it at school.

Sergeant Cleary offered me an oatmeal biscuit.

'We're not having a go at you,' he said gently. 'You do a top job, coping with him. We understand it's a tough call for a kid, having an embarrassing dad, that's all.'

I ignored the biscuit.

I didn't ignore the vicious insults about Dad.

I grabbed a sheet of paper off the desk and wrote on it in big letters so they'd understand.

'MY DAD IS THE BEST DAD IN THE WORLD. IF YOUR WIFE DIED, YOU'D PROBABLY TRY TO CHEER YOURSELF UP BY WEARING BRIGHT SHIRTS AND SINGING COUNTRY MUSIC TOO.'

Sergeant Cleary and Constable Pola looked up from the sheet of paper and exchanged a glance. I could see they'd never thought about it that way before.

Sergeant Cleary pushed about six biscuits into my hand and steered me out the door.

'I haven't told your dad about this,' he said. 'I didn't want him coming down here and singing at me.'

He went back into the police station. If I could, I would have shouted after him that Dad doesn't sing at just anyone, only when he's feeling really moved.

I thought about putting it in a note and leaving it under the windscreen wiper of the police car.

I didn't, because what Sergeant Cleary had said was starting to sink in.

He hadn't rung Dad.

Dad didn't have to know what had happened.

I was still standing there, weak with relief, when a woman got out of a van and came over to me.

'Rowena?' she said.

She was tall and blonde and wearing posh clothes and for a millionth of a sec I had a totally and completely dopey thought.

That Mum hadn't died after all, that she'd just lost her memory and wandered off and now she'd got it back and here she was.

Then I remembered that Mum wasn't tall and blonde. In the photos in Dad's album she was shorter than him, with dark hair. And she had smiling eyes.

This woman was smiling, but her eyes weren't.

'Hello,' she said. 'I'm Paige Parker.'

Of course. That's where I'd seen her before. On telly, on that current-affairs show.

I saw the van she'd just got out of had a TV logo on it.

'You been having a bit of a run-in with the police?' she asked.

I didn't know what to say. I was confused. If Paige Parker and her TV crew were filming a story on Mr Wetherby as one of the oldest surviving diggers in the state, why was she interested in me?

Then I twigged. Mr Wetherby isn't much of a talker, not since his teeth got a bit loose. Ms Parker must be looking for other local person-alities to pad out her story. People with World War One relatives and quiet teeth. The police must have given her my name. Kids with bits missing always get heaps of viewer interest, specially if they're into crime.

Except I'm not into crime. Not really. I had to explain that to Ms Parker before I was branded a crim on national TV.

I handed her the police biscuits and pulled out my notebook.

'I was just getting Dermot Figgis to back off,' I wrote, 'like our soldiers did to the Germans in World War One.'

I handed her the page and waited for her to thank me for linking my explanation to her story about Mr Wetherby.

The cameraman was getting out of the car. Perhaps she was going to thank me on camera.

Then I realised what a total and complete idiot I was being. I snatched the page back from her and turned and sprinted down the laneway next to the police station.

'Rowena,' I heard her yelling. 'Wait.'

I didn't.

I ran across the supermarket carpark, round the back of the newsagent and hid in the fruit shop's big waste bin.

It was pretty revolting in there. Today's a public holiday so it hadn't been emptied since yesterday and the heat had made all the fruit and veg scraps go mushy.

It was like I was being punished for what I did to Dermot Figgis's car.

But I stayed in there till I was sure the TV people had gone.

If I'd appeared on TV, Dad would have seen it and then he'd have known about Dermot's car and me being hauled in by the cops.

Dad works very hard at being a good dad. He's not so hot on punishment and discipline, but he does it if he thinks he has to.

He'd really think he had to if he heard about the car and the cops. Which would totally and completely ruin what's left of Mum's special day.

I wish I didn't have so much cabbage slime in my shoes. It's hard to walk fast with soggy socks and I want to get home as quickly as I can so Dad and me can get back to being really close and I can forget about all the crook stuff that's happened today.

Oh no, I've just had an awful thought.

The TV people probably know where I live.

Dermot Figgis certainly does.

It's not over yet.

I hurried into our driveway and stopped dead.

The hairs on the back of my neck stood up. Or they would have done if they hadn't been sticky with peach juice and mushy cauliflower.

A strange car was leaving the house and coming towards me.

My brain twitched with fear but it didn't switch off.

Who was it?

One of the TV people?

Dermot Figgis in a hire car?

Luckily our driveway's really long because it goes right through the orchard, so I had time to duck behind a tree before the car got close.

As it bumped past I had a look inside. There was only one person, a bloke a bit older than Dad with black curly hair and a suit.

Dermot Figgis's lawyer?

A TV producer who'd been to see Dad about the screen rights to my life of crime?

I hurried up to the house, my chest tight and not just because the watermelon juice in my T-shirt was drying all stiff.

Claire was in the kitchen washing up and keeping baby Erin amused with the timer on the oven.

'G'day, Ro,' she said. 'What's that in your hair?'

I looked at my reflection in the oven door.

'Lettuce,' I said. 'Don't worry, I'm planning to hose it off.'

Claire grinned. She's got really good at understanding sign language since she married Dad. Less than a year and she knows 'planning'. Not bad.

Erin gave a big chortle and pointed to my head. Two-month-old babies think soggy lettuce on the scalp is the funniest thing they've ever seen.

'Who was that who just left?' I asked, trying to keep my hands steady.

Claire hesitated, but only for a sec.

'Bloke Dad used to know,' she said. 'He's passing through town. Dropped in for a cuppa.'

I concentrated on tickling Erin under the chin so Claire wouldn't see how relieved I felt.

'Dad's outside,' said Claire. 'Spraying the back paddock.'

I wasn't surprised to hear that. Dad always has a spray on Mum's anniversary. Spraying perks him up when he's feeling down. He sprays on the day his mum died, too, and every time a big bill arrives. When Erin peed on his Carla Tamworth records, he sprayed for about six hours.

I took a deep breath and hoped there hadn't been any other visitors before the one I'd seen. TV journalists, for example, or motor-vehicle insurance investigators.

I went out to the back paddock. Dad was on the tractor. He must have fixed it because it was hauling the big blower up and down the rows of trees as good as new.

Dad looked at me through the misty clouds of spray.

I looked back anxiously, trying to tell whether he was angry or upset. I couldn't see his face. When Dad sprays he pulls his cowboy hat down over his eyebrows and ties a scarf round his nose and mouth. He reckons it's just as good as a spray suit and doesn't make him feel like a Martian.

I could tell from the way he was sitting that everything was OK. Dad's one of those people who, when they've heard something that makes them angry or depressed, their shoulders sort of hunch up and they hardly ever steer a tractor with their feet like Dad was doing now.

I felt wobbly with relief.

Dad waved and told me to stand back while he finished spraying.

'OK,' I said. 'Then we'll get the album out and look at photos of Mum.'

That's another good thing about having a dad who can speak with his hands. You can have a conversation even when he's got a scarf over his mouth and you've got a two hundred horsepower blower roaring away next to your ear.

I stood back and watched Dad blasting the root weevil, plus any blue mould, codling moths and apple scab that happened to be in the area.

They wouldn't have known what hit them.

Just like I didn't know what hit me a few minutes later.

Dad finished the last row, switched everything off and strolled towards me, tipping his hat back and pulling his scarf down.

'G'day, Tonto,' he said. 'I was worried about you. Thought Dermot Figgis might have clogged up the car wash and flooded the town.'

My insides dropped, but only a little way because Dad was hugging me so tight.

How did he know about Dermot's car?

Then I saw the empty trailer, still caked with bits of rotten apple, sitting in the corner of the paddock.

Of course. Mr Lorenzini must have told him.

I looked anxiously up at Dad.

'Good one, Tonto,' he said proudly, grinning down at me.

I gaped at him. I almost asked him to say it again with his hands in case the blower had damaged my eardrums.

'That'll teach Dermot Figgis to mock the memory of a fine woman,' continued Dad. 'I've rung Mrs Figgis and told her that if Dermot's got a problem with what you did, he can come out here and I'll hose his car out myself. Then I'll do his mouth.'

I sagged against Dad's chest, dizzy with relief.

'And I rang Sergeant Cleary, too,' Dad went on, 'and told him that next time he decides to lock you up, I want to know pronto. I asked him why he hadn't rung me, but he wouldn't say. Just kept saying it didn't matter cause he'd already released you. I reckon he's a ratbag.'

I grinned into Dad's shirt.

'Here,' said Dad, stepping back and rummaging in his pocket, 'I want you to have this to help you pass the time if you find yourself in the slammer again.'

He pulled out his hanky and unwrapped something silver and shiny.

It was a mouth-organ.

Dad blew a few notes and handed it over.

'It was my grandfather's,' he said. 'His mates sent it home after he was killed in the war.'

Then Dad launched into a Carla Tamworth song about a bloke sitting in jail waiting for his sweetheart to turn up so he can prove he didn't murder her. She turns up eight years later because it's taken her that long to finish the tunnel she's dug to rescue him.

I tried to play bits of the tune, but I didn't do a very good job. It's not easy, playing a harmonica when your throat's all lumpy with happiness.

Has any kid in the history of the world had such a completely and totally top dad?

No way.

The rest of the day was perfect.

Well, almost.

Me and Dad and Claire cooked a fantastic dinner. Claire put chopped onion in the apple fritters and they tasted better than they ever have in my whole life.

Claire was great the whole evening. It's only her second anniversary of Mum, and these occasions can be pretty tough for a new wife.

She handled it brilliantly, even when Dad got a bit carried away and went on about what a great talker Mum was. He told the story about the time he invented an apple-polishing machine and his dad's pit bull terrier fell in and its face got polished so much it lost most of its fierce looks and Mum persuaded the local RSPCA officers not to prosecute Dad even though Grandad really wanted them to.

'She won 'em over just with words,' said Dad, misty-eyed. 'Didn't need to use beer or apple pies or anything, the Gab didn't.'

Mum's family name was Gable before she was married, and because she was so good at stringing words together, Dad used to call her 'the Gab'.

'That must be where Ro gets being such a great talker from,' said Claire, smiling at me. 'The gift of the Gab.'

That's the nicest thing anyone has ever said to me with their mouth. I'm making my pillow damp now, just thinking about it.

I reckon Mum would be glad that Dad's got a top person like Claire for a new wife. And a top baby like Erin for a new daughter. She'd reckon he deserves to be happy.

And I agree with her.

Which is why I'm so worried about the phone call this evening.

Dad answered it, and when he'd hung up he turned to us, his face alarmed and a bit disbelieving like he'd just heard someone had invented a tractor that could fly.

'That TV mob that was at the ceremony this morning,' he said, 'they want to film me tomorrow for their show.'

Claire hugged him. She looked concerned too.

'How do you feel about that?' she said.

Dad glanced at me. He must have noticed I was feeling anxious too.

'OK,' said Dad, 'I s'pose.' He frowned, then gave a sort of grin. 'Perhaps I'll get my own series.'

Normally if he said something like that, Claire would tickle him till he begged for mercy. This time she just chewed her lip.

I tried to look on the bright side.

Sergeant Cleary must have given the TV people Dad's name as a colourful local personality with a relative who died in World War One and good teeth.

Which is fine except for one thing.

Some people can feel really hurt if unkind things are said about them on national TV.

Things like 'one of the biggest ratbags in the district'.

It was worse than I'd feared.

I tried to keep them away.

I got up really early and stuck a big sign on our front gatepost. 'Danger,' it said. 'Root Weevil Plague. Keep Out.'

They ignored it. Their van just roared up the driveway. Perhaps TV people aren't very good at reading.

By the time I got up to the house, they were already talking with Dad in the lounge-room.

I pressed my ear to the door, trying to hear what they were saying. It was no good, I couldn't catch a word. Erin was crying in her room and she's loud enough to drown out tractors with holes in their mufflers.

Then Claire hurried into Erin's room and the crying stopped.

I pressed my ear to the door again.

'Cock-eyed,' I heard Dad say. 'Totally and completely cock-eyed.'

Claire appeared, jiggling Erin.

'Ro,' she said. 'Fair go. How's a bloke meant to be his sparkling best in an interview when he's being eavesdropped on?'

I lifted my hands to protest, but Claire just grinned.

'Anyway,' she continued, 'you won't miss anything. The minute they've gone he'll be dancing around telling us everything he said.'

I went outside and did some digging.

Digging's my best thing for stress. There's something about shoving a spade into dirt that really takes your mind off tension and worries.

I'm digging Erin a sandpit. It's a surprise for when she's old enough to hold a bucket. Up till today it hasn't been a very big sandpit because I haven't been stressed that much lately.

It's pretty big now, but.

And I still couldn't stop worrying.

What had Dad meant by 'cock-eyed'?

Was he saying he'd rather be described as cock-eyed than a ratbag?

Or had he just been telling his funny story about when he sang a country and western song at his uncle's funeral and the congregation just stared at him cock-eyed, mostly because he was at the wrong funeral?

36

The more I dug, the more I reckoned it was the funny story.

Finally I heard the TV people drive off in their van.

I raced indoors, grabbing my mouth-organ off the verandah in case Dad wanted some music played while he entertained us with the best bits of his interview.

He didn't.

I could tell from the way he was sitting slumped forward. And from the way Claire had her arms round him and her head against his neck.

My insides went splat like an over-ripe apple.

'What happened?' I asked.

Dad had his face in his hands and Claire was staring at the floor, so they didn't hear me.

I knelt down in front of them.

Claire jumped. She seemed alarmed to see me. She gave Dad an anxious nudge.

'Didn't the filming go well?' I asked.

'They didn't do any filming,' said Claire. 'They want to do it later in the week.'

'Eh?' I said, using the special sign me and Dad have worked out for a stunned pit bull terrier staggering out of an apple-polishing machine. 'Later in the week? But Anzac Day was yesterday. Why are they taking so long to do the segment?'

'Turns out,' said Dad quietly, 'the sneaky

mongrels didn't come to town to film an Anzac Day segment. They came to film me.'

I stared at Dad while I digested this.

For a sec I hoped his distraught expression was just from the stress of being a star and wondering which belt buckle to wear.

It wasn't.

'Or rather what I should say,' said Dad angrily, 'is that they came to film a heap of cock-eyed lies and nonsense.'

He stood up and stormed out of the room.

His bedroom door slammed.

I started to go after him. Claire grabbed me.

'Let me talk to him first,' she said. 'Please.'

I didn't take much persuading because I've got something even more important to do.

I'm on my way to do it now.

That's one of the great things about talking with your hands. You can run all the way into town and then yell at someone straight away without having to catch your breath.

How dare Paige Parker try and get a mean cruel comedy segment out of a great dad just cause he's a bit eccentric.

Anyway, why shouldn't an apple farmer sing country and western songs? Country and western singers are allowed to have apple trees.

Let's see what Paige Cheese-Brain Parker has to say about that.

I know where she's staying.

Posh TV people don't stay in cheap motels or caravan parks, and there's only one posh motel in town.

I just wish it wasn't Mrs Figgis's.

I thought I knew the worst thing that could happen at Mrs Figgis's motel.

I thought it was if Mrs Figgis caught me and made me hose out Dermot's car.

Boy, was I wrong.

What happened was much worse than that.

I was scared Mrs Figgis would be at reception, so I didn't go there to ask which unit Paige Parker was in. Motel owners have to spend long hours at the reception desk in case the guests try and steal the pens.

As it turned out I didn't need to ask. I guessed a TV star would be in the Honeymoon Suite cause it's got a spa and a microwave.

At least I was right about that.

I crept across the carpark towards the Honeymoon Suite, ducking down behind the cars so I couldn't be seen from the office.

Suddenly a car door opened and almost bashed me in the head.

A grown-up got out of the car.

It was Mrs Figgis.

'Rowena Batts,' she said loudly.

I froze, wishing there was a very deep sandpit nearby so I could bury myself.

There wasn't.

'Um . . .' I said. 'Er . . .'

My hands flapped helplessly.

It's really hard making excuses when the other person doesn't understand sign and you can't think of anything to say even if they did.

'You poor kid,' said Mrs Figgis. Except she didn't sound very sympathetic. 'I think what your father did to you is a disgrace.'

I stared at her.

What did she mean?

'No wonder you do crazy things,' said Mrs Figgis, glaring at me angrily. 'I'd want to kill him if I was you.'

I started to back away, wondering if the pressure of living alone with Dermot had made her go mental.

'It's OK,' she said, 'I know who you're here to see. Go on, she's in 23.'

I hurried over to the Honeymoon Suite before Mrs Figgis snapped and attacked me with her shopping bag.

Paige Parker opened the door while I was still bashing on it.

Her face relaxed and she put her hand on my shoulder. 'Rowena,' she said, 'what a nice surprise. Come in. Come in.'

I went in.

'Have a seat,' said Paige Parker.

I didn't. I went over to the big mirror on the wall, picked up a lipstick from the clutter of makeup on the bench, and wrote in big letters on the glass, 'LAY OFF MY DAD.'

'Rowena,' said Paige Parker, 'we have to talk.'

I glared at her. Nobody tells me to talk if I don't want to.

I tore a page out of my notebook and handed it to her. The writing wasn't great because I'd done it while I was running into town, but she could still read it.

'It's not fair,' it said. 'Dad had an unhappy childhood. Now he's a top dad. Don't make fun of him.'

Paige Parker gave a big sigh.

On the TV next to her a video was playing. On the screen white mice were running around in cages. They were pretty weird mice. Some had no tails. Others didn't have enough legs. She was probably planning to make fun of them next.

'Rowena,' said Paige Parker, 'there's something I have to tell you.'

She sat on the settee and patted the cushion next to her.

I stayed standing.

'This isn't going to be easy for you to hear,' said Paige Parker softly, 'but I sense you're a person who would rather know the truth.'

Suddenly the sound of her fake-friendly voice and the smell of her perfume was making me feel a bit queasy.

What was she going to tell me?

That Dad once got into a fight with Mr Cosgrove at a community service night and pushed his face into a bowl of avocado dip?

That Dad once jumped up on stage at a Carla Tamworth concert and sang a song to me even though the whole crowd was chucking stuff at him?

I knew that.

I knew everything she could tell me about Dad.

That's what I thought.

Boy, was I wrong.

'Rowena,' said Paige Parker in a soft voice, the sort of voice people use to speak to very little kids. 'I'm not doing a story about eccentric dads. I'm doing a story about the chemical sprays that farmers use on their crops.'

Suddenly I felt better. Dad's an expert on sprays. He uses heaps. He's always giving other farmers advice about them. He'd be perfect for a segment on sprays as long as he didn't try and talk with his scarf over his mouth.

That's what I thought.

'To be more exact,' continued Paige Parker, 'I'm doing a story on farmers who use sprays in a harmful way.'

She pointed to the TV screen. The poor mice with bits missing were still scampering around.

'These mice,' said Paige Parker, 'were all born with physical problems. All for the same reason. Before they were born their mothers were exposed to large amounts of chemical farm spray.'

I stared at the TV, my head spinning. It was the most outrageous accusation I'd ever heard.

'My dad's never hurt mice,' I said angrily. 'We haven't even got mice on our farm.'

I could tell she didn't understand me, but that didn't stop her. She picked up a fat wad of photocopied pages and looked straight at me.

'University tests,' she said, 'have shown that sprays can hurt people as well. If their mothers were exposed to lots of spraying, people can be born with physical problems too.'

Suddenly I was feeling very queasy.

'Your dad,' she said, 'does a lot of spraying.'

Suddenly I couldn't breathe.

Then I realised what's happened.

This is Mrs Figgis's revenge for what I did to Dermot's car. She's told the TV people a whole lot of made-up lies about Dad and sprays. She's forged university documents. She's found a video of mice who've been in car accidents. She's made it look like it was Dad's fault I was born with bits missing from my throat.

I tried to explain all this to Paige Parker. I tried to explain that the doctors have always said that my throat was probably a genetic problem I got from Mum or Dad. I tried to explain that me and Dad had our yearly medical check-up only two months ago and the doctors said we were as fit as fleas.

My hands were shaking so much with rage and indignation I could hardly write.

Paige Parker made me sit down.

She told me she's got some other evidence. 'Gold-plated' was how she described it.

I'm letting her show it to me.

We're driving there now in the TV van.

I'm not worried, but.

It'll be as ridiculous as all the other stuff.

But it's important I see it. It's important I see exactly what vicious hurtful lies Mrs Figgis and Paige Parker have cooked up between them so I can get Paige Parker sacked from her job and Mrs Figgis run out of town.

I don't want to think.

I don't want to remember what I've just seen.

I just want to lie here under this tree and look up at the leaves. If I keep staring at the leaves, I won't have to remember.

It's no good.

I can't get the pictures out of my mind.

I've seen some pretty bad paddock damage in my time. From drought. And bushfire. And truck mud-racing. Once at school I saw a photo of what a war can do to an orchard. But I've never seen anything like what Paige Parker showed me today.

When we got out of the TV van I just stared.

It was a big paddock and once it would have had fruit trees.

Now it's just got rows of withered tree skeletons standing in a wasteland of dead grass.

Not burnt.

Not drought-affected.

Not bombed.

Just dead.

'A few weeks ago,' said Paige Parker, suddenly using her TV voice, 'this was a normal healthy orchard. Then we had it sprayed.'

'What with?' I whispered.

My hand-movements were so small she couldn't have understood even if she'd known sign, but she must have seen in my face what I was asking.

'We used a lot of different sprays,' she said. 'Including, for purposes of scientific research, sprays now on the danger list. Sprays that farmers were still using in this district up until about ten years ago.'

I realised Paige Parker had paused, and was staring at me intently.

'Farmers,' she said, 'including your father.'

When I heard this, the tree skeletons started to wobble in front of my eyes and not just because I was standing in the sun.

Then I had a thought.

'How come,' I wrote shakily on my notepad, 'our orchard doesn't look like this?'

I held the notepad up so Paige Parker could read it.

'Because,' she said, 'we used more chemicals than even the most enthusiastic farmer would use. We wanted to show viewers just what this stuff can do. So they can make up their own minds. About whether these chemical cocktails have the power to tragically ruin the lives of young Australians like you, Rowena.'

I stared at the paddock. No fruit. No leaves. No birds. Not even any insects.

I've seen Paige Parker do heaps of segments on TV.

Her facts have always seemed pretty good to me. They've never looked to me like she's cooked them up with a revenge-crazed motel proprietor.

What if she hasn't now?

What if these ones are true?

Suddenly I felt weak and had to hold on to the fence.

Then I snatched my hands away in case they'd sprayed that too.

Paige Parker put her hand on my shoulder.

'I'm sorry we had to show you this, Rowena,' she said, not softly but loud as if she was speaking to several million people. 'We felt you deserved to know the truth.'

Even though my eyes were full of tears, I noticed the cameraman was filming me.

If I could, I would have screamed 'STOP!' But I couldn't, so I ran.

I dashed across the road and jumped into a gully and sprinted along a dry creek bed so they couldn't follow me in the van.

I heard them running after me for a bit. Then the cameraman tripped over something, went sprawling and swore.

'It's OK, Mike,' I heard Paige Parker say, 'we've got enough.'

I kept running for ages until I came to this tree.

It's a huge tree and it's very green, but even several million leaves aren't enough to distract me.

My chest's hurting.

It's hurting partly from the run and partly from the awful thought I'm having.

The thought that if Paige Parker is right, and Dad did use too much spray before I was born, then he could have caused a terrible, terrible thing to happen.

He could have caused Mum to die.

As I ran home, trying to keep tears out of my eyes so I didn't crash into trees, I knew exactly what I wanted Dad to do.

I wanted him to get a microscope and a bloodhound and a team of private detectives and come up with some evidence of his own.

Evidence to prove he didn't use too much spray when I was inside Mum.

Evidence to prove he didn't make my throat turn out crook.

Evidence to prove he didn't kill Mum.

'Dad,' I wanted to beg him after I burst into the house. 'Prove they're wrong. Prove you didn't do it. Please.'

But I couldn't.

He was sitting at the kitchen table, shoulders slumped, staring at a slice of toast. He'd probably been there since the TV people left this morning.

He looked so unhappy I couldn't make him feel worse.

How would he have felt, his own daughter demanding proof and not trusting him?

So I just clenched my guts into a small tight knot and said, 'I know you didn't do it, Dad.'

He hugged me so tight that the fringe on his shirt left little dents in my cheek.

'I'd never do anything to hurt you, Tonto,' he whispered.

He hugged me for so long that Claire got worried about dehydration and made us a cup of tea.

It was a kind thought, but I needed more than tea.

What about Mum? I wanted to ask, but I couldn't.

And then, when Dad had wiped his eyes and built up his strength with a cuppa and a mouthful of toast, he told me without being asked.

His evidence proved everything I wanted it to prove, everything I needed it to prove so our lives could go back to being the same.

Except that by the time Dad had finished, my life had changed totally and completely for ever and ever.

I'm lying here on my bed and my brain feels like someone's been bashing it with the wardrobe.

It's in shock.

It can't take everything in.

Perhaps if I start at the beginning and go through it all again slowly, it'll cope better.

First Dad opened his cardboard expanding file, the one he keeps all his Carla Tamworth fan-club newsletters and other important documents in. It was already on the kitchen table instead of under the bed where he usually keeps it.

'This,' he said, 'was my bible.'

He slid a crumpled piece of paper across the table to me. It was covered with numbers written in biro, dirty thumbprints and what looked like a couple of squashed flies.

'This was given to me fifteen years ago,' said Dad, 'by the top agricultural chemical bloke in the state.' He took the piece of paper back and smoothed it out carefully, eyes shining like it was a satin shirt he'd found in the two-dollar bin at the op-shop.

'Every squirt of spray I used in those days,' said Dad, 'I bought from Stan. And I stuck to his instructions like it was the holy book.' Dad pointed to the numbers on the paper. 'How much. How often. How much water to mix in. Look, he even wrote down how thick my rubber gloves should be.'

Claire was standing behind Dad, rubbing his shoulders.

'Those old-time salesmen really knew their

stuff,' she said. 'It was their whole life. My dad sold stationery. He could name eleven different types of paper clip.'

I was so relieved to see Dad's evidence I wanted to snatch the piece of paper and cover it with kisses.

I didn't, partly because of the squashed flies and partly because there was something really important I had to ask Dad.

I took a deep breath.

'Dad,' I said, 'how did Mum die?'

I first asked him that when I was seven and he held my face gently in his hands and said, 'Peacefully, soon after you were born.'

I didn't ask for more details because he was crying at the time and I didn't want to upset him more.

Also I had a terrible suspicion her dying might have had something to do with me being born, so I didn't want more details in case they upset me more.

Now, suddenly, this arvo, I did want more details.

Dad was looking pretty strong, staring at that piece of paper, and I felt he could probably cope.

Boy, was I wrong.

He shut his eyes and his shoulders slumped even lower.

'Jeez, Tonto,' he said with such tiny hand-movements it was like he was whispering,

'I've done a terrible thing.'

I stared at him in panic.

Oh no, I thought. Please don't say you were so besotted with love for Mum that you forgot to check your bible and you accidentally mixed up a lethal dose of spray and a cloud of it floated into the house while Mum was only wearing undies.

Please don't say that.

Dad took a very deep breath, then sighed and let his hands drop onto the table.

Claire hugged him and stroked his hair.

'Tell her,' she said quietly to Dad. 'You'll have to sooner or later.'

Dad nodded.

He looked at me and his face was scared.

Then he got up from the table and went out of the kitchen and I heard him go into his bedroom and open the wardrobe.

For a sec I thought he was going to hide in it. When a pet cockatoo I used to have ripped Erin's room to shreds before she was born, I felt like spending the rest of my life in my wardrobe. I would have done if the cocky hadn't ripped it to shreds too.

Dad came back into the kitchen.

He was still looking scared and he was carrying an old cowboy-boot box.

'Rowena,' he said, and took another deep breath.

I took one too.

He only calls me that when things are really serious.

'Rowena,' he went on, his voice wobbling, 'I haven't told you the truth about how Mum died.'

I tried to swallow but my mouth felt drier than an over-sprayed paddock.

Dad took the lid off the boot box and lifted out some old newspaper cuttings. He put them on the table. I studied them, desperately hoping I wouldn't see any words like 'lethal dose of spray' or 'only wearing undies'.

The cuttings were yellow and the print was faded. For a sec I thought that's why I couldn't read them. Then I realised they were in a foreign language.

'Rowena,' said Dad, 'Mum was knocked down by a car in France.'

I stared at him.

'France?' I said, once my hands had regained the power of speech. 'France the country?'

'We were on a trip,' said Dad quietly. 'Me, Mum and you. Two months after you were born. We were staying in an old town with narrow streets. A car was going too fast . . .'

He stopped.

I felt like I was trying to breathe under stewed apples.

'The car hit her,' he whispered. 'It hit her and didn't stop. She was killed.'

His hand was trembling as he touched a blurry photo of Mum in one of the cuttings.

Claire was biting her lip and stroking his hair.

I just sat there, stunned, my whole life changed.

How could he do it?

How could he lie to me all this time?

After a bit, another question forced its way into my thoughts.

'Did they catch him?' I asked.

Dad shook his head.

'Some people reckoned they knew who it was,' he said. 'A local. But there was no proof. And you know how overworked police are in country towns. And anyway, what did it matter, she was dead. I was just so grateful it wasn't worse.'

I didn't understand.

Wasn't worse?

'How could it have been worse?' I yelled so loudly I knocked over the tomato sauce.

His eyes suddenly filled with tears.

'She could have been holding you,' he said. 'I was holding you, but she could have been.'

He put his arms round me and I started crying too.

After a while I pulled away.

'Why didn't you tell me?' I asked.

Dad stared at his hands.

'You were a kid,' he said, 'and . . . and I

didn't want you brooding about it all. I just wanted you to be happy.'

Then Claire put her arms round us both and murmured something to Dad about a tape.

Dad took an old walkman cassette out of the boot box and handed it to me.

'I recorded this in France,' he said. 'The day before Mum was killed.'

I stared at the tape.

For a sec I thought it was going to be Dad singing.

Then Claire explained.

Which is how come I'm lying here on my bed holding a tape of my mother's voice.

A voice I've never heard.

All my life I've tried to imagine it. A warm, soft, gentle voice. A strong, cheeky, laughing voice.

A loving voice.

And now, when at last I'm able to hear it, I'm scared.

But I'm going to do it now.

I'm putting the tape into my walkman.

I'm switching it on.

Now I understand.

Now I know why Dad's nuts about Carla Tamworth.

One of Australia's top country and western singers sounds just like my mum.

Except my mum's got a better voice.

I can't stop saying it.

My mum.

Singing just for me. Well, that's what I'm pretending.

The tape's pretty confused at first. Just heaps of loud voices talking over each other in French. That must be why Dad's never given me the tape before. It would have been a total and complete giveaway about France.

There's loads of clinking. Sounds like they're in a pub. Either that or an apple-sauce bottling factory.

Dad drops the tape player at one point and

says 'poop' and spends ages fiddling with the microphone.

Then a man makes an announcement in French and people clap. Either that or the place has got a tin roof and it starts to rain.

Then Mum starts to sing and the place goes quiet.

I'm not surprised.

She's brilliant.

She sings a country and western song about a dingo trapper who breaks his leg in the desert. He can't walk so his faithful old dog drags him back to town. It takes a week because the dog is caught in a dingo trap and she's got to drag that too.

There's a bit the trapper says in the chorus that gets to me every time.

'I know you love me
I know you're doing your best,
That's why I'm not angry
You've got my head in an ants' nest.'

Each time I play it my chest goes all tight with love for her.

I've had to stop playing it, partly because my chest's hurting and partly because I don't want to wear the tape out. It's got to last me for the rest of my life.

Erin's just started crying in her room.

I reckon she's going to have a voice just like Mum's.

I wish it could have been me.

I wish I could have had Mum's voice.

Instead of just a mouth-organ.

But I'm not going to think about that because I've got something much more important to think about.

Somewhere in a village in France is the bloke who killed my mum.

Free and alive and unpunished.

I've got to think how I can change that.

I've got to think how I can get to France and find him and prove he did it and bring him and his car to justice.

It won't be easy.

I'm lying here thinking of all the practical parts of it and I feel like my head's in an ants' nest too.

But one thing's for sure.

I'm going to get the mongrel.

I lay awake for hours wondering how a person with ninety-seven dollars in her savings account can get to France.

A garage sale?

A raffle?

A bank loan?

Trouble is, I can't tell anyone why I need to go. People just don't buy raffle tickets or give bank loans for missions of revenge.

Plus Dad wouldn't let me go. He hates me missing school. And he obviously thinks bringing a murdering hit-and-run driver to justice is too dangerous or he'd have done it himself.

At 2 a.m. I still hadn't solved the problem of how to get to France so I got up for a dig. I have some of my best ideas while I'm digging.

Except this time I didn't get to do any.

I'd just collected the spade off the verandah when Dad appeared wide-eyed at the back door.

'Rowena,' he said. 'No.'

He lunged towards me and grabbed the spade.

'You don't have to do that,' he said. 'I admit it. Mum isn't buried in the town cemetery, she's buried in France.'

I stared at him in horror.

His body sagged inside his Carla Tamworth pyjamas.

'Mum's grave here is just a pretend one,' he said miserably. 'A kind of memorial. I'm sorry, love.'

I felt sick.

All these years I've been visiting the wrong grave.

Then I stared at the spade in Dad's hands and felt even sicker.

He thought I was going to dig up Mum's grave to see if it was real.

'Dad,' I said weakly, 'I was only going to dig a sandpit.'

I took him down the garden and showed him.

There was an awkward silence. I could tell Dad was embarrassed he'd thought I could do such a thing. But grown-ups never really know what kids are capable of. Specially when it comes to catching hit-and-run drivers who've killed their mums.

'Dad,' I said, 'I want to go to France to visit Mum's real grave.'

I was telling the truth. I do want to visit it. I want to cut the grass on it and put fresh flowers on it and kneel down on it and tell her I've dealt with the mongrel who killed her.

Dad crouched down in the moonlight and studied the hole.

'Good-sized sandpit,' he said.

'Dad,' I said, sticking my hands in front of his face. 'Please. Take me to France.'

'It'll need a fair whack of sand,' said Dad.

I grabbed him and shook him. He grasped my hands and held them tight.

'Not now,' he said. 'One day, but not now.'

I tore my hands free.

'Why not now?' I demanded.

Dad hugged himself even though it wasn't the slightest bit cold. Maybe polyester satin pyjamas aren't as warm as they look.

'I can't afford it,' he said, 'and you've got school and I've got to deal with these TV clowns and Erin's too young to travel and . . .'

I interrupted him.

'You took me to France when I was as young as Erin,' I said.

Sometimes parents dig holes for themselves that are even bigger than sandpits.

Dad sighed.

'That was different,' he said. 'Mum's mum was living in Canada. You were her first grandchild. She sent us plane tickets so we could take you over there to show her. Mum arranged for us to stop off in France on the way back cause I'd never seen my grandfather's war grave.'

'So,' I said, 'you know how it feels to really want to see a grave.'

'I didn't want to see it,' he said. 'Mum made me.'

I was very close to hitting him with the spade.

'Tonto,' he said, 'I do know how you feel, but it's just not possible now. We'll go in a year or two, cross my heart and hope to get blue mould.'

'It's not fair,' I said bitterly.

But actually I wasn't that bitter because Dad had just given me another idea.

I know how I can get to France.

It won't be easy and I'll have to wag school tomorrow, but if I can pull it off I'll be on the plane in a week.

Grandad was killing ants when I arrived.

'Mongrels,' he was yelling at them.

He stood on his front step whacking them with a broom that was almost taller than he was.

Then he saw me and glared, panting. His skin was bright red under the white bristles on his face and head.

I felt like a little kid again. It used to really scare me when I was younger and Grandad's face would suddenly go red, usually from yelling at Dad or ants.

Grandad took a step back. 'Who are you?' he said. 'What do you want?'

I stood there, dumb.

I hadn't expected that.

It wasn't much of a welcome from my only living grandparent. Specially after I'd travelled three towns down the highway and walked forty-five minutes from the bus-stop.

'What's the matter?' demanded Grandad. 'Cat got your tongue?'

He didn't recognise me. I was confused. He couldn't have lost his marbles, he's only eighty-one. Mr Wetherby's ninety-eight and he knows the names of all his great-grandchildren and their Telly Tubbies.

Then it hit me. I hadn't seen Grandad for three years. People can change a lot in three years. He hadn't, but I had. My hair was much lighter three years ago.

I hunted in my bag for a piece of cardboard and my texta. I could have booted myself up the bum. On the bus I'd written the things I needed to say to Grandad on bits of cardboard and I'd completely forgotten to do one introducing myself.

I did a quick one now and held it up to him.

'I'm Ro,' it said. 'Your granddaughter.'

He stared at it for a long time. I wondered if I should write another one saying 'Your son Kenny's girl'.

Then he grinned. 'Rowena,' he said. 'Jeez, you've grown. Still dumb, but.'

I nodded and gave him a rueful shrug to show him it's no big deal.

He thought of something and glared again.

'Did that no-hoper son of mine send you?' he growled.

I shook my head. I didn't bother going into

more detail on a piece of cardboard. Grandad knows Dad hates him and doesn't want to see him. From the scowl on Grandad's face I could tell he felt the same.

Instead I found the first message I wrote on the bus and held it up.

'G'day, Grandad,' it said. 'I've come to ask you a very big favour.'

Grandad read it and scowled again.

'I'm not seeing that bludger son of mine,' he said. 'Not till he apologises.'

I sighed. This was what I'd feared. I was hoping we wouldn't get sidetracked into Dad and Grandad's war, but Grandad obviously still feels as strongly about it as Dad does. The last time they saw each other, Christmas three years ago, Grandad had too much homemade alcoholic cider and yelled at Dad and Dad called him a booze bucket and a viper-mouthed old troll and a pathetic excuse for a father.

It's tragic. I've even heard Dad talking about Grandad in the past tense, i.e. 'my dad's name *was* Clarrie', as if he'd carked it.

I decided to write another card explaining to Grandad that my visit had nothing to do with Dad.

Before I could, Grandad grabbed my hand.

'Hungry?' he asked.

I shook my head. I'd had an apple fritter walking from the bus-stop.

'Bulldust,' said Grandad. 'Kids are always hungry.'

He dragged me into the house. It was gloomy inside and smelt of old blankets and bacon. As I followed him down the passage I tried not to think about what might be waiting for me in the kitchen. It's not Grandad's fault. When people live alone and have to get through whole loaves of bread by themselves, life must be a continual race against blue mould.

In fact the slices he cut me looked pretty fresh. And the butter was from the fridge. I started to relax.

'Do you like jam?' said Grandad.

I hesitated, wondering how long the average solo pensioner takes to get through a jar of jam. Particularly one who prefers homemade cider to spreads.

'Course you do,' said Grandad. 'All kids like jam.'

He opened a new jar of apricot and spread it on the bread really thickly. I realised I was pretty hungry after all.

Then Grandad went over to the stove, picked some pieces of cold bacon out of a fat-congealed pan, laid them carefully on the bread and jam, shook tomato sauce onto the bacon, put the top of the sandwich on and slid it towards me.

'My favourite,' he said.

My stomach tried to hide under my liver.

Don't get ill and offend him, I told myself. Remember why you're here.

I took a deep breath, silently asked Mum to wish me luck and held up the next piece of cardboard.

'Can you take me to France,' it said, 'to see my mum's real grave?'

Even before Grandad had finished reading it, his face twisted into a snarl.

'France?' he spat. 'I wouldn't go to that dung heap if you paid me a million dollars.'

I hoped he was just grumpy because I wasn't eating the sandwich.

I pressed on with the next card.

'I'll pay you back for the plane ticket when I'm older,' it said.

'If you go to that death-trap of a country you won't get to be older,' snapped Grandad. 'My father went there and was killed. Your mother went there and was k . . .'

His voice petered out. He obviously wasn't sure if Dad had told me the secret about Mum. Then his voice came back.

'If you think I'm setting foot in France,' yelled Grandad, 'your brain's as dud as your throat.'

It wasn't looking good, but I wasn't despairing. I still had one more card.

I held it up.

'You could visit your dad's war grave,' it said.

'Why would I want to do that?' growled Grandad.

I stared at him, shocked.

Poor bloke. His dad was killed before he was born. It's tragic when a kid doesn't even get to meet a parent. If only his dad had left a tape of himself singing a country and western song.

Then I remembered the mouth-organ.

I took it out of my bag.

'This was your dad's,' I wrote on a piece of cardboard. 'Would you like it?'

Grandad stared at the mouth-organ, face going bright red again. Then he grabbed it and threw it into my bag.

'Get out,' he said. 'How dare you come here upsetting an old bloke. You're worse than your ratbag father. Out!'

He grabbed me and pushed me down the passage and out of the house and slammed the door behind me.

I stood in the front yard, shaking and indignant.

He could have just said no thanks.

For a sec I wanted to yell at him that he was a viper-mouthed old troll, but the cardboard was probably too thick to push under his door so I didn't.

I turned sadly and headed back to the bus-stop.

About fifty metres down the road I heard his voice.

'Rowena,' he was shouting, 'wait on.'

I turned, my heart doing a skip, and saw him hurrying towards me.

Yes, I thought, he's changed his mind. He's remembered the life-insurance money he got when grandma died and he's decided to spend it on getting closer to the father he never knew.

I held out my hands to give Grandad a hug.

He held out his hands too.

In them was a soggy paper bag.

'You forgot your sandwich,' he said.

This bus ride home is taking forever. If it doesn't reach town soon I might have to eat the sandwich.

At least it's giving me time to think.

Poor Grandad, not being able to get revenge for his dad's death. That's the crook thing about wars. You can't bring people to justice because they're allowed to kill each other.

Poor Dad, growing up with such an angry father. I reckon Dad's done a pretty good job, turning out so different. I'd rather have a dad with a bright-red shirt than a bright-red face any day.

I just wish he'd told me the truth about Mum.

I sort of understand why he didn't, but. He knew the most important thing was for me to feel close to Mum. He knew how far away France would seem to a kid.

He was right, it does seem far away.

Every time I try and think of a way of getting there, it seems further.

But I've got to get there.

If I can't think of a legal way soon, I might have to do something really desperate.

And I don't mean eat the sandwich.

As I hurried along the road to our place, I was so busy worrying how I could get to France I didn't notice the purple thing standing by our gate till I almost bumped into it.

Dermot Figgis's car.

My guts went tight.

I ducked behind a tree and crouched in some undergrowth.

The car was standing with all its doors open. The cow-pattern seat covers were spread out on the roof. The Simpsons car mats were on the bonnet.

Heart thumping, I wondered if Dermot had come to take my hairdryer so he could dry out the car quicker.

Tough luck, I thought. I haven't got a hairdryer.

Then I heard voices.

I peered through some couch grass and saw

Dermot and another bloke squinting up our driveway.

'Doesn't look any different,' said the bloke doubtfully. 'Looks the same as any other orchard.'

'It's a chemical bombsite,' said Dermot. 'Makes the Iraqi oilfields look like a national park. That's what the TV crowd told my mum.'

'Ripper,' said the bloke, scribbling in a notebook. 'If I can get that clown Kenny Batts to talk I'll get a front page out of this.'

Suddenly I recognised the bloke. Stan Gooch, a reporter with the local paper. He plays footy in the same team as Dermot Figgis. And there was Dermot, dobbing Dad in to him. Spreading lies and hurtful gossip.

I very nearly let Dermot have it. The bloke on the farm next to ours keeps horses and I could have had Dermot's car full of horse manure if they'd kept talking for another hour or so.

I didn't, but.

It was more urgent to warn Dad. Having your name dragged through the mud on national TV is bad enough, but on telly there's always the hope that people will be watching a video or changing the oil in the tractor when it's on.

Everyone round here reads the local paper.

I crept back down the road, jumped the fence, ran through the orchard and burst in through the back door.

'Where's Dad?' I said to Claire, who was

doing some paperwork at the kitchen table. 'The local paper's after him.'

Claire took a moment to understand my hand-movements. Then she gave a groan. 'Not the local paper as well,' she said. 'You'd better warn him. He's in the big shed.'

Typical Dad, I thought as I hurried out to the shed. When things get tough he always likes to keep busy. Probably changing the gaskets in the apple-polishing machine.

At first I couldn't see him in the gloom of the shed.

I pulled out the mouth-organ and played a few notes. Hand-movements aren't much use attracting someone's attention if they've got their head up an apple-chute.

'Over here, Tonto,' he called out.

He wasn't changing the gaskets in the apple-polishing machine. He wasn't even picking dust out of the grease nipples. He was sitting in the corner of the shed behind a pile of apple boxes eating a bacon and jam sandwich.

'Those TV mongrels have been trying to get me on the blower all day,' he said. 'Thought I'd be safer out here in case they turn up in person.'

He didn't say the word but I knew what he was doing.

Hiding.

I was shocked. Dad never hides from trouble.

All my life he's faced up to it and usually sung it a song.

Now he looked so sad and stressed I didn't know what to say.

I told him I'd do the same thing in his position. It wasn't true, but he'd lied about Mum to save my feelings so I thought it was only fair.

I took a deep breath and wished I didn't have to tell him about the local paper.

As it turned out, I didn't.

Claire came into the shed carrying Erin and her bankcard. She held the card out to Dad.

'Take it, love,' she said. 'Go to France till this blows over. Please.'

My heart started thumping so loudly I thought for a minute the apple-polishing machine had switched itself on.

Say yes, I begged him silently. Even if you don't want to, say yes for Mum.

Dad stood up.

'Thanks, love,' he said, 'but I'm not blowing all our savings. I'm staying here to fight the mongrels.'

My guts felt like stewed apple sliding down the inside of a car windscreen.

Claire sighed. 'You're going to fight the local paper as well?' she said.

I could see this rocked Dad. He hesitated for a bit, and when he spoke his voice was much quieter than it usually is.

'I can't leave you here with the bub,' he said. 'It'd be different if we could afford tickets for all of us.'

Claire gave a grim smile.

'I'll be OK,' she said. 'I've handled worse than a few pesky journalists.'

She has too. She used to be a teacher and once she took Year Six on a camp.

Dad was still hesitating.

I was holding my breath.

Claire looked hard at Dad, flicked her eyes towards me and back to Dad. She didn't think I saw it, but I did.

'I think you should,' she said to Dad.

Dad put his arms round her and the baby and buried his face in her hair.

'OK,' he mumbled.

'Yes!' I wanted to shout, but of course I couldn't.

I gave Claire a hug too, and told her she's the best step-mum in the history of the world, including Hollywood.

We've been making travel plans all evening. There's heaps of arrangements to make. We're going to drive to the city tomorrow and make them there, where the local paper can't find out about them.

My guts are in a knot.

I've been lying here in bed for hours, playing Mum's tape and thinking about what I've got to do when I get to France.

I feel like my head's in an ants' nest again.

It's pretty normal though, eh, not being able to sleep the night before a big trip.

Most people have that trouble, even when they're not planning how to catch a murderer.

I think the crew are onto me.

The flight attendants have been giving me strange looks ever since we got on the plane.

I saw two of them whispering to each other just now.

'The girl in 58B,' I think one said, 'she's planning to ruthlessly hunt down a French criminal and make the French police look lazy and slack. We'd better alert the French authorities.'

I hope I'm wrong.

I hope they're just staring because of my mouth-organ. I was playing it a bit loudly during takeoff. I needed something to help me relax and you can't dig on a plane.

My worry, but, is that they're staring because of the security-alarm incident.

It wasn't fair. Nobody warned me that a mouth-organ would set off the metal detector at the airport security gate. I'd have put it through the x-ray machine with Dad's belt buckle if they had.

Instead I had to take everything out of my pockets, including the plastic car and the rag doll I've borrowed from Erin's toybox.

Dad gave me a puzzled look when he saw them. He knows I haven't played with dolls for years, and I only play with cars when he wants a race.

I'm hoping he's thinking I've just borrowed them to remind me of Erin. Instead of to help me act out Mum's death for the jury in a French courtroom.

The security guards saw them too, and swapped a look.

I reckon they told the flight attendants.

It'll be tragic if I get stopped now, because everything's gone so well over the last three days.

We drove down to the city without any problems except for one scare when we saw a van behind us. We thought it was Paige Parker but it just turned out to be a nappy service.

The travel agent in the city was really helpful, specially when we gave him a box of apples. And the passport office, where we thought we might have to queue for days, was a breeze. They've got a special counter for handicapped people, and because Dad's finger was in a splint after he shut it in a cupboard door at our motel, we felt OK about using that.

It was the busiest three days of my life. I hardly had time to think, let alone worry about being sprung.

I've only started worrying about that since we've been on the plane.

If only I could tell Dad what I'm planning to do. At least then if the French customs officials handcuff me and try to bundle me on a plane home, he could protest to the Australian embassy.

But I don't want to make him more stressed. He's got enough on his plate as it is, poor bloke. The pressure of being unfairly hounded by the media's really getting to him.

Usually he wears his best clothes when we're going somewhere special. His pink satin shirt with the black guitar on the back and his Viking-on-a-tractor belt buckle.

So far this trip all he's worn are denim work shirts and the World War One belt buckle he only wears when he's depressed.

Usually if he was in a group of three hundred bored people he'd have a sing-song going by now. There's a Carla Tamworth song about a bloke sitting on a rock waiting for his pilot sweetheart to arrive for their wedding. He doesn't know she's crashed and he waits so long that moss grows on his tuxedo. It'd be perfect for a twenty-two-hour flight like this one.

But Dad's just sitting here, flicking through the in-flight magazine.

I offered him a go on the mouth-organ, but he just shook his head and –

Oh no, a flight attendant's bending over and speaking to him.

Is she explaining that I'll have to be sent home at Singapore?

No, she's just asking Dad to tell me not to play my mouth-organ once they start the movie.

Phew, they mustn't be onto me after all.

That's a relief.

Now I can relax for the rest of the flight.

Except for one other little thing that's worrying me.

When we were saying goodbye to Claire and Erin at the airport, Claire whispered something to Dad. She didn't think I heard because I was busy blowing a raspberry on Erin's bottom, but I did.

'Ro's old enough to know the full story,' she whispered to Dad.

The full story about what?

I asked Dad while we were waiting to get on the plane, but he just looked away and mumbled something about showing me the exact place where Mum was killed.

I had the weird feeling he was hiding something.

I hope not.

Perhaps I'm just getting too suspicious after everything that's happened.

Can't be helped.

You need to be a bit suspicious when you're tracking down your mum's killer.

We got through French customs without a hiccup.

OK, one.

On his customs form, under 'Reason For Visit', Dad put 'holiday'. On mine I put 'business'.

It was careless of me, but luckily they just thought I was a dopey kid who didn't understand forms.

Still, I wanted to get out of that airport fast, in case their computer matched my name with Mum's name and they saw I was the daughter of an unsolved hit-and-run victim planning to take the law into her own hands. I know Mum's death was quite a few years ago, but computers can do that sort of thing standing on their heads.

'Airport train station,' said Dad. 'This way.'

I've got Claire's rucksack and Dad's got a

suitcase on wheels so we can move pretty fast.

We're here, I thought, my insides tingling with excitement. We're in France and I'm going to avenge Mum and nothing can stop me now.

Boy, was I wrong.

First, we got lost. Paris airport is like a huge shopping centre. Dad always gets lost in shopping centres, even ones that don't have signs in French.

We bought a French phrase book and found the station.

Then Dad tried to buy tickets.

The bloke in the ticket office couldn't understand what Dad was saying and Dad couldn't understand what the bloke was saying.

Dad said the name of Mum's town all the different ways he could think of, but the ticket bloke just kept frowning.

'Sorry, Tonto,' muttered Dad. 'It's been twelve years since I've said it.'

I handed him the phrase book.

The phrase book didn't have towns.

'Tell you what,' said Dad to the ticket bloke. 'Show me a list of all your towns and I'll see if I can spot it.'

The ticket bloke looked at him blankly.

Dad started thumbing through the phrase book.

I started feeling pretty anxious in case the ticket bloke decided to run a check on us. Train ticket-office computers are almost as powerful as customs ones.

Then I had an idea.

I rummaged in my rucksack until I found the old French press cuttings about Mum. Without letting anyone see them, which wasn't easy because there were about fifty angry people behind us in the queue, I copied down all the words in them that started with capital letters.

I showed my notebook to the ticket bloke, praying that one of the words was the name of the town.

The ticket bloke rolled his eyes and put two tickets on the counter. He said something in a loud voice. It was in French but I got the gist from his hand-movements. He was saying I was smarter than Dad, which I thought was pretty unkind in front of all those other people.

Then he said something else.

I watched his hands closely.

'We've got to change trains in the city,' I said to Dad.

'I knew that,' said Dad grumpily. 'I'm not an idiot. I only did this trip twelve years ago.'

The station we changed at in Paris was the biggest station I've ever seen.

I gaped, even though I've promised myself I won't get distracted from my mission of revenge by tourist sights. There was a roof over the whole station, and the noise of pigeons and trains and French people echoed like something in a dream. And the air smelled fantastic, like apple fritters made with garlic.

Dad brought me down to earth quicker than a sprayed codling moth.

'After we've had a squiz at Mum's grave,' he said, 'we'll go to Euro Disney.'

He pointed to a huge poster of Mickey and Goofey riding on a roller coaster with French writing coming out of their mouths.

I stared at him in panic.

Why would a bloke who's just travelled round the world to his dead wife's grave want to go to Disneyland?

Must be jet-lag.

'Um . . .' I said, trying desperately to make my hands look natural, 'I'm feeling pretty jet-lagged too so I wouldn't mind resting-up in Mum's town for a bit first. Just for a couple of weeks.'

Dad gave me a strange look. I don't know why, I was telling the truth. I hardly slept at all on the plane. Every time I nodded off, I clunked my head on the woman next to me's crossword book. It's OK for Dad, he can sleep anywhere, even on a tractor.

We're on the train now, and I'm staring out the window at the French paddocks. They're even flatter than ours at home. And really dark green, except for the ploughed ones, which are dark brown.

A few minutes ago a thought suddenly hit me.

I'm only a few miles away from Mum.

Maybe the colours just seem darker because of that.

They can do, when you've got tears in your eyes.

Then I had another thought. As far as I can see, the French paddocks are bare of trees. There are a few trees around the houses and villages, but they don't look very friendly.

'Is Mum buried near apple trees?' I asked Dad anxiously a moment ago. I really hoped she was. At least they'd remind her of home.

'No,' said Dad. 'Too wet round here for apple trees. All they can grow round here is turnips.'

That's really crook.

My own dear mum, buried near turnips.

That mongrel driver's gunna pay for that.

It's not fair.

All I needed was a few days.

Once I was on the hit-and-run driver's tail I could have tracked him down really quickly. Specially if he'd panicked and left clues lying around.

I could have had a written confession by Thursday, probably.

Instead all I got was twenty minutes.

Twenty minutes in Mum's town before the police swooped.

Twenty minutes and here I am in the back of a police car.

They probably spotted me and Dad when we came out of the station. We must have looked pretty suspicious, the way we were staring at everything.

Dad was staring at street signs, trying to remember the way to the hotel. He was also glancing anxiously at every passer-by.

At first I couldn't work out why he was doing that. Then I twigged. He must have been worried the locals would recognise him as Mum's husband. And think he'd come back to stir up trouble about her death.

If things turned ugly he couldn't run very fast because a wheel had fallen off his suitcase. That must be why he was trying to hide his face with his jacket collar, which is about as suspicious as a person can look in public, specially when they're wearing cowboy boots in a district that doesn't have any cows.

I can't blame it all on Dad, but. I was probably looking pretty suspicious myself with all the staring I was doing.

I was staring at how narrow the streets are. No wonder people get knocked down here. And you can't even widen these streets because all the houses and shops are made of brick. At home if you want to widen a street you just bung the wood and fibro buildings on the back of a truck and shift them back a bit.

I was staring at the streets for another reason too.

I was wondering which one Mum was killed on.

I kept getting a pang in my chest and it wasn't just the rucksack strap cutting into me.

For a bit I wasn't sure if I really wanted to know.

Then I remembered it was a clue and I had to know.

I was about to ask Dad when he suddenly pointed to a damp-looking grey building.

'Our hotel,' he said.

I don't understand why the police didn't just pick us up on the street. Why did they wait till we were in the hotel? Perhaps they needed to go to the toilet before they arrested us.

I certainly did.

I left Dad at the check-in desk thumbing through the phrase book and went for a pee.

When I sat down I realised how tired I am. I haven't slept for about twenty-six hours. I almost nodded off on the dunny.

I stopped myself, but, and when I got back to the check-in desk Dad wasn't there.

I looked around.

I saw the police car parked outside.

I saw an anxious face peering at me through the car window.

It was Dad.

For a sec I thought I'd nodded off and was having a nightmare.

I hadn't.

This isn't a dream.

We're in a police car and the policeman behind the wheel is driving much too fast down these narrow streets.

He must be taking us to police headquarters.

Well, I won't be blabbing.

They can shine a lamp in my eyes and question me for hours, but it won't do them any good.

All I'll tell them is my name, my address and what class I'm in at school.

Talk about weird.

I mean, I know France is a foreign country, but I wasn't prepared for anything like this.

The police car suddenly stopped outside a brick house with blue shutters on the windows and a hedge that had been carved into shapes of birds and windmills and things.

Jeez, I thought, pretty strange police headquarters.

It got stranger.

The policeman beeped the horn and two people came running out of the house. One was another policeman. He had a moustache and a tummy that wobbled as he ran and a feather duster. The other was a tall woman in normal clothes. I figured she must be a detective. She was wearing an apron, but I've heard how much French people like to cook.

As they got closer to the car, I noticed a really strange thing.

They were both grinning and waving at me and Dad.

They both looked really excited to see us.

All I could think of was that it had been ages since they'd had anyone to interrogate and they'd been getting really bored.

Then Dad got out of the police car and the policeman with the tummy threw his arms round Dad.

The woman detective did the same.

Dad looked a bit taken aback and I got out of the car in case this was a form of police brutality I hadn't come across in Australia.

It wasn't – they were hugging him.

The woman hugged me too, and even though I didn't have a clue what was going on, it felt pretty nice.

'Rowena,' she murmured. 'Little Rowena.'

She let go of me and I stared at her.

Her voice didn't sound like a detective at all. It was so beautiful it made my neck prickle. It was the warmest, softest, gentlest voice I'd ever heard. I wondered if all French people sound like that when they speak English.

'Rowena,' said Dad, 'this is Mr and Mrs Bernard. They're mates of mine.'

Normally I can cope with just about anything Dad comes out with, but today I just stood there staring at Mr and Mrs Bernard like a stunned aphid.

Mates of his?

Mrs Bernard was gazing back at me.

She had tears in her eyes.

'Poor girl,' she murmured. 'Poor, lovely girl.'

I wondered if she meant me.

Mr Bernard was talking excitedly at Dad in French, waving his feather duster. I tried to work out from his feather-duster movements what he was saying. Something about a telephone.

'My husband does not speak English,' Mrs Bernard said to me.

I nodded. My brain was still too scrambled to say anything intelligent.

The policeman who'd driven us was carrying our bags into the house. Mrs Bernard put her arm round my shoulders and gently steered me along the gravel path to the front door.

Mr Bernard was still talking excitedly.

'Alan is saying we are sorry we didn't meet you,' Mrs Bernard said to Dad, 'but when the hotel rang us we were unprepared. Why did you not let us know you are coming? Why the secret hotel?'

I could see Dad didn't know what to say, even in English.

Perhaps Mrs Bernard's voice had got to him too.

'Er . . .' he said, 'um . . . we were gunna surprise you.'

I had a feeling he was making that up, but I didn't dwell on it because suddenly I had something else on my mind.

Something so big and so confusing that I tripped over Mrs Bernard's feet and almost fell into a bush shaped like a car.

I would have done if Mrs Bernard hadn't caught me.

The thing is this.

If Dad is such big mates with the local police, why didn't he get them to track down Mum's killer?

I'm sitting on the bed in the little attic bedroom Mrs Bernard has brought me to and I'm trying to figure it out.

I can't.

When Dad came in to check my bed was comfy and to see if his toothbrush was in my rucksack, I asked him.

He looked away with a pained expression.

At first I thought he hadn't heard me because he'd just remembered he'd used his toothbrush on the plane to polish his boots.

But he had heard me.

All he did, though, was give me a big hug and say, 'Sometimes, Tonto, it's best to let things rest.'

Well, he might think so, but I don't.

I thought about the mystery for ages, which wasn't easy with jet-lag.

If Dad had wanted to, he could have got Mr Bernard and the other local police to check every car in the district for hit-and-run dents.

They could have done it standing on their heads.

Why didn't they?

I didn't know, so I went downstairs to look for clues.

Dad and Mr and Mrs Bernard were in the kitchen. As I came along the passage I heard Dad saying, 'I want to tell her myself.' Then Mrs Bernard said something in French, which was probably her translating for Mr Bernard.

I went into the kitchen and they all stopped talking.

Dad went down on one knee and sang me a quick verse of that haunting Carla Tamworth classic 'I Love You More Than Pickled Onions'.

When he'd finished I was about to ask him what it was he wanted to tell me himself, but Mrs Bernard spoke first and what she said took my breath away, and not just because of her voice.

'We go now to your mother's grave,' she said. 'Yes?'

My guts gave their biggest lurch since our plane hit an air pocket over Afghanistan.

I nodded.

We piled into another police car with Mr Bernard driving this time and soon we were speeding through the narrow streets.

My chest was thumping so hard from fear and excitement that I didn't think about flowers till we were almost out of town.

I prodded Dad and told him.

'Bit late for flowers now,' he said. 'Sorry, Tonto.'

I was stunned. Normally Dad would crawl through wet cement to get flowers for Mum's grave.

Mrs Bernard turned and gave me one of her sad smiles. 'It's not too late,' she said. 'Ro must have flowers.'

She said something to Mr Bernard in French and he slammed on the brakes and did a squealing U-turn through a petrol station. He zoomed back into town and parked on the footpath outside a flower shop.

Inside, Mrs Bernard said lots of things in French to the two young women shop assistants. While she spoke they stared at me, their eyes getting bigger and bigger.

It didn't worry me, I get stared at quite a lot.

I just wanted to buy some flowers and get to my mum's grave.

The assistants must have understood my hand-movements because suddenly they jumped into action and gave me a beautiful bunch.

Then something weird happened.

They wouldn't take any money. Even when Dad took the senior assistant's hand and put some French money into it she just gave it back.

He tried again with Australian money, but she didn't want that either.

I realised what was going on.

They probably hadn't seen a kid before with bits missing from her throat.

'They're being charitable,' I said to Dad.

Dad frowned and turned to Mrs Bernard, who was smiling and nodding. He opened his mouth to explain how Australians don't usually accept charity unless it's absolutely essential because we're used to battling a harsh land with droughts and bushfires and floods and unreliable tractors and pushy TV presenters.

Then I saw him decide it was too complicated to try and explain all this through a translator, even a top one like Mrs Bernard.

Instead he gave me an apologetic shrug.

It was OK, I understood.

Well, I thought I did.

'Ta muchly,' Dad said to the assistants. 'Very nice of you.'

That's what I thought too, at the time.

Mr Bernard got us to the cemetery in about three minutes.

Mum's French cemetery is very different from her Australian one. It's got a wall round it with a gate, probably to keep out local hoons and their dog poo.

I was shaking so much as I followed Mrs Bernard through the gate that I could hardly hold the flowers.

She took me to Mum's grave.

Most of the graveyard is gravel, and most of the graves are grey stone.

Mum's isn't, but.

Mum's is the most beautiful grave I've ever seen.

Her headstone is marble and her grave is covered with really soft dark-green grass, perfectly clipped and edged with more marble.

But it wasn't just the neatness of the grass that made my mouth fall open.

It was the four other bunches of flowers lying on it.

All fresh.

I stared, gobsmacked.

I'd imagined Mum's French grave would be wild and unkempt and I'd be the first person tidying it up and putting flowers on it for twelve years.

Instead it's the best-cared-for grave in the whole cemetery.

I was about to ask Dad what was going on when something else happened. An elderly couple standing at another grave with a poodle looked over and saw us and gave a shout. They hurried over and started shaking Dad's hand and beaming. Dad looked a bit alarmed, probably because the poodle was trying to have sex with his leg. Even though I couldn't understand a word the French people were saying, I could see they were delighted.

Why?

Was Dad being mistaken for a local footy star? Surely not with his crook knees.

Then it hit me.

The reason everyone here is so friendly to Dad.

The reason nobody's bothered to catch the hit-and-run driver.

The thing Dad wanted to tell me himself.

The full story Claire reckoned I should know.

It's this.

Dad must have been offered a deal when Mum was killed.

The local council must have offered Dad a top grave for Mum, serviced regularly, if he agreed not to make them hunt down the hit-and-run driver.

And he accepted.

That's why all the locals are so grateful to him. He's saved them the shame and embarrassment of admitting they've got a ruthless killer in their municipality.

Of course. That's why Dad wanted to sneak into town without anyone knowing we were here.

He was scared a local would blab to me.

He was scared I'd lose all respect for him.

Which is exactly what I'm doing.

Dad, how could you?

How could you let a killer get away with it for a bit of lawn and a few flowers?

That's what I asked myself at the cemetery as I laid my flowers on Mum's grave and it's what I'm still asking back here in Mrs Bernard's attic bedroom.

I haven't asked Dad in person.

I don't want him to know I've twigged.

He might guess what I'm planning to do and try to stop me.

Not that I'd let him.

I'm going to avenge Mum even if it means the local council won't look after her grave any more and I'll have to live here for the rest of my life and mow it myself.

It was morning and Mum was stroking my forehead and talking to me softly in her warm gentle voice with its warm gentle French accent.

French accent?

I opened my eyes.

It wasn't morning, it was night and it wasn't Mum smiling down at me, it was Mrs Bernard.

'Sweet little Rowena,' she whispered.

I wish she wouldn't keep saying that. I'm not little and when I get my hands on a certain local driver I don't plan to be sweet.

'You slept for five hours,' said Mrs Bernard. 'Now you need food.'

It was a kind thought but she was only partly right.

I also needed clues.

'We go to the cafe,' said Mrs Bernard.

My heart gave a skip of excitement.

I jumped out of bed and splashed water on

my face from the bowl so Mrs Bernard wouldn't see my mind racing.

Cafes are good for clues, I was thinking. People gossip in cafes. It's the milkshakes. Sugar loosens tongues as well as teeth, that's what Dad always reckons. In cafes down our way people are always mentioning the names of other people who've been mean to pets or overdressed at the bowling club or driving carelessly.

Hope it's the same here, I thought as I brushed my hair. Hope French cafes are good for clues.

This one was.

Sort of.

Mr Bernard drove us there in about ninety seconds, which was pretty scary because it was round at least twelve corners.

The trip was nowhere near as scary as the cafe itself.

Inside there wasn't a single milkshake.

Just smoke and noise and music.

And people.

About a hundred people, all raising their glasses of wine and beer to us and cheering as we walked in.

I glanced at Dad. He looked as stunned as I felt. But he soon started to relax as people shook his hand and slapped him on the back and yelled at him in excited and happy French.

Probably thanking him for sticking to the deal.

Boy, I thought bitterly as people shook my

hand too, and patted my head, and gave me glasses of mint cordial. Do French people a favour and they never forget it.

Dad hasn't been in this town for twelve years and people were falling over themselves to buy him a drink. We were only away from our town for five years while I was at the special school and when we got back people didn't even remember us.

I wished Sergeant Cleary was in the cafe tonight. He'd soon change his opinion of Dad if he saw how popular Dad is in France. I even thought of ringing him and telling him. Then I remembered I've lost respect for Dad, so I didn't.

Mr and Mrs Bernard steered us through the crowd to a table at the back. We sat down and almost immediately someone put big plates of meat stew in front of us.

I was starving and even though it's not easy eating a meal while about fifty people are staring at you and grinning and your guts are knotted with lack of respect for your father, I gobbled it down.

Right up until I had a thought.

I looked around at the faces and suddenly I wasn't hungry any more.

Any one of those men, I realised, could be the hit-and-run driver.

The men carried on grinning and saying friendly-sounding things.

The meat stuck in my throat.

Mrs Bernard slapped me on the back and anxiously lifted my glass of mint cordial to my lips.

She's a very kind woman, but if she really wanted to help my digestion she would have given me a name, not cordial.

Then, as soon as Dad finished eating, everybody started shouting at him.

Mrs Bernard whispered something to him and he stood up and cleared his throat and did his neck exercises.

That could only mean one thing.

They wanted him to sing.

I was speechless.

Dad's sung to big groups of people heaps of times but tonight was the first time I'd ever seen a group ask him to.

He climbed onto a table in the middle of the cafe and sang the Carla Tamworth song about the bloke with ninety-seven cousins who loves them all dearly even though he can't remember any of their names.

The crowd went wild, even though Dad didn't get many of the notes right.

Then he sang Mum's song.

I realised I was probably in the actual place where Dad had taped Mum singing it all those years ago.

Suddenly my eyes were full of tears.

Which is how I came to turn away, so people wouldn't see.

Which is how I came to spot the man with the black curly hair.

I noticed him at first because he was the only person not standing gazing up at Dad. He was putting his coat on and heading for the door.

Either he's late for something else, I thought, or he's got musical taste.

Then I recognised him.

I'd seen him before, in Australia.

He was the bloke driving down our driveway when I got back home from being locked up at the police station.

What's he doing here?

I yelled at him to wait, but he wasn't looking in my direction so he couldn't see my hands.

As he opened the door several of the people in the cafe waved goodbye.

I struggled through the crowd, but by the time I got to the door and peered up and down the street, he'd gone.

My head spun in the cold night air.

If he's a local, what was he doing at our place in Australia?

I asked Dad on the way back to Mr and Mrs Bernard's.

Dad reckoned I was mistaken.

He reckoned it must have been someone else.

It wasn't, but.

I've been lying here in bed for ages testing my memory and I know I wasn't mistaken.

He's the same bloke I saw in our driveway. He even had the same suit on tonight. What's going on?

When I woke up and realised it was really early, I had a listen to Mum's tape. Just a few times so I didn't wear it out.

I'm glad I did. I reckon Mum's voice inspired me. In less than twenty minutes I'd thought up a complete two-part investigation plan.

Part One. Start at the beginning and find the exact spot in town where Mum was knocked down.

Part Two. Try and find a passer-by with a really good memory who'd been walking a pet nearby at the time of Mum's death and could remember the number plate of the car.

OK, Part Two was a bit hopeful, but I'm still glad I thought of it, given what's happened since.

'Dad,' I said at breakfast. 'Where exactly was Mum killed?'

Dad sighed and looked unhappy, though that

might have been because Mrs Bernard had left a dried goat's cheese on the table and Dad had just put the whole thing in his mouth thinking it was a muffin.

'Tonto,' he said, using his hands, 'don't torture yourself.'

I thought that was pretty rich coming from a bloke who was choking to death on his own breakfast.

I poured him a glass of water.

'Rowena,' he continued, 'I want you to stop thinking about Mum's accident, OK?'

I gave him a look I hoped would curdle cheese.

He looked at his hands, which I could see were struggling for the right words.

'She didn't suffer,' he said at last.

There was pain on his face and it wasn't just from the cheese and suddenly I felt sorry for him.

'She heard the car,' continued Dad with trembling hands, 'and tried to get out of the way. She slipped. The car whacked her on the back of the neck. It broke her spinal cord. The doctors said she died instantly. There, now you know.'

I fought back tears.

I had more important things to do than get sad.

'Did you see the car?' I asked.

Dad shook his head. 'It was dark and raining

and I was busy with you,' he said.

The tears wouldn't go away. Not now I was thinking that if I hadn't been there, Dad might have been able to save her.

'We've got to stop this,' said Dad. 'We both need a good cheer up. Tomorrow we'll say goodbye to this dud place and I'll take you to Euro Disney.' He took a deep breath through his nose and gave me a cheesy grin. 'Couple of weeks there and we'll be doing cartwheels back to Australia.'

I didn't argue.

When Dad gets an idea in his head it's like couch grass. Takes weeks to shift.

I haven't got time.

After Dad had gone back to his room for a lie down to finish swallowing the cheese, I tried Mrs Bernard.

'Mrs Bernard,' I wrote, 'do you know which street my mother was killed in?'

Mrs Bernard studied my notebook.

She gave a huge sigh.

For a sec I thought it was because I'd ended a sentence with 'in'. Then Mrs Bernard hugged me to her chest so tight I was worried her bra strap was going to make one of my eyes pop out.

'My poor, poor little Ro,' she said. 'Don't make yourself tortured.'

I realised she'd been talking to Dad. She sat me down and went to the fridge and made me a huge ice-cream sundae with peaches and frozen raspberries and mint syrup.

It was very kind, but I took it as a 'no'.

I tried Mr Bernard.

He was in his workshop out the back, wearing a white singlet and braces, cleaning a rusty old pistol with a cloth. On the workbench were lots of other rusty old pistols and rifles. A few clean ones hung from the roof with some cheeses.

When Mr Bernard saw me he smiled and said something in French. Then he mimed digging.

For a sec I thought he was asking if I was feeling stressed. I was about to tell him I was, but that I didn't have time to dig a sandpit. Then I realised he was telling me the guns had been dug up. From battlefields, I guessed. There were heaps.

Before he could go into lengthy detail about the war, I showed him my notebook.

Mr Bernard looked at it blankly.

I hoped desperately French policemen were trained to read English even if they couldn't speak it.

Mr Bernard shrugged apologetically.

I wished I had a better phrase book. All the phrases in the one I've got are for talking to hairdressers and waiters. You'd think a decent phrase book could translate a simple sentence like, 'Do you know in which street my mother was killed?'

Then I had an idea.

I beckoned to Mr Bernard and he followed me through the house to the front yard.

I pointed to the bush that had been clipped into the shape of a car. Then I pointed to another one that was shaped like a person. I couldn't tell if it was meant to be a man or a woman, but I hoped he'd twig I was talking about Mum.

Mr Bernard frowned, then his face lit up.

He dashed into the house.

Yes, I thought. He's gone to get a map of the accident location. Or maybe even a file with a list of suspects' names in it.

Mr Bernard reappeared, waving a pair of hedge clippers.

My insides sagged like an apple fritter in cold oil.

Then, while I was politely watching Mr Bernard clip a bush into the shape of a kangaroo, it hit me.

Of course. Clippings. Newspaper clippings.

Finally Mr Bernard finished and I thanked him and hurried up to my room. In the phrase book I looked up the French word for street.

Rue.

Then I pulled the old French newspaper clippings about Mum's death out of my rucksack. There, in the first one, I found them. *Rue Victor* and *Rue Amiens*, both in the same sentence.

I checked another one. *Rue Victor* and *Rue Amiens* again.

I could hardly breathe.

Mum must have been killed at the corner of those two streets.

I stuck my head and hands into Dad's room, trying not to look too excited. Dad was cleaning his teeth. I hoped he'd bought a new toothbrush.

'I'm just going for a walk,' I said.

Dad gave me a doubtful look.

'The tourist office might have Euro Disney brochures,' I said.

Dad thought about this, then nodded. 'Don't be long,' he said.

On a notice board in front of the town hall I found a tourist map with a street index.

Rue Victor and Rue Amiens were only a few minutes away.

When I finally arrived here on the corner where they run into each other, possibly on the exact spot Mum was killed, I felt very sad.

And then, when I looked around, very angry.

Yes, Victor and Amiens are narrow streets, and yes it was night when Mum was killed, and yes it was raining.

But there's a street light right over the corner. Not a new one, it's at least fifty years old, so it would have been there on that night. And a pedestrian crossing. And stop signs.

That driver must be a maniac.

My eyes filled with angry tears. Through the blur I noticed a young woman in pink jeans on the opposite corner giving me a strange look. I turned away and found myself staring into the window of a deli.

That's when I saw the most amazing thing I've seen in my life.

The window was full of sausages and meatloaves and slices of devon and jars of meat sandwich spread. Except that in the middle of the display was a pile of dried dog poo.

The same type of dried dog poo that Dermot Figgis left on Mum's Australian grave.

It couldn't be.

I blinked and pressed my face against the window.

I've got really good eyes. When one bit of you doesn't work, the other bits get extra good, it's a known fact.

I've been staring at that stuff in the deli window for ages now.

It's definitely Dermot's dog poo.

Except sausage shops don't put dog poo in their window, that's also a known fact.

So it can't be dog poo, it must be a type of sausage.

Which is even more amazing.

Why would Dermot Figgis leave two French sausages on my mother's grave?

Before today I thought hit-and-run clues were things like dented bumper bars and bent aerials and people selling their cars for $11.50.

Not dog-poo sausages.

Boy, was I wrong.

But it took me a while to realise it.

I was still staring at the sausage-shop window, trying to remember if Dermot Figgis and his mum had been on holiday to France recently, when a man came out of the shop.

He was wearing a white apron and carrying a big leg of ham that was the same pinky-white colour as his bald head.

With a warm smile and a little bow, he gave me the ham.

I staggered under the weight of it, not knowing what to say.

Then I remembered what Dad's always told

me about taking gifts from strange men, so I gave it back to him.

A woman with a grey hairdo came out of the shop. She was wearing a white apron too and holding a big salami on a string. She kissed me on both cheeks and gave me the salami.

Dad's never said anything about accepting gifts from strange women, but he's pretty strict about no charity so I gave the salami back.

It's incredible.

There must be a shortage of people around here with bits missing. When one comes along, the kind people in this town go bananas.

I realised I'd met the man and woman before. At Mum's cemetery yesterday. And at the cafe last night. They were kind there too. When Dad finished singing they applauded longer than anyone else, despite the fact that they must both be in their fifties and a bit short of energy.

Now they were looking really disappointed that I didn't want their gifts.

I was glad there was one thing I did want from them so I didn't have to disappoint them completely. I pointed to the dog-poo sausages in the window.

Their faces lit up and they led me into the shop.

The man reached into the window, lifted the whole pile of sausages onto a sheet of white paper and held them out to me.

I took one.

I didn't want to do what I was about to do, but I had to be sure.

I sniffed it.

It didn't smell like dog poo.

I rolled it next to my ear.

It didn't sound like dog poo.

I bit a piece off and chewed it.

It was hard and dry and as it crumbled between my teeth, strong flavours filled my mouth.

Salty flavours. Garlicky flavours. Spicy flavours.

None of them were dog-poo flavours.

It was definitely a sausage.

I must have been grinning with relief because the man and the woman both started grinning too.

'Moth-hair,' said the man. For a sec I thought he meant the sausage was made from moth hairs. I wished I hadn't just swallowed some. Then I realised he was saying 'mother'.

'Fav-oo-reet,' he said. I understood. This sausage was his mother's favourite. Then I saw he was pointing to me and my stomach went cold.

He was saying the sausage was *my* mother's favourite.

'Deedoh,' he went on, nodding and smiling. 'Australee.'

The woman gave him an anxious dig with her elbow, but he didn't seem to notice.

I stared, brain churning, as he mimed packing the sausages into a suitcase, climbing onto a plane, flying to Australia, unpacking the sausages and laying them very carefully onto the ground.

'Moth-hair,' he said again. 'Fav-oo-reet.'

With a gasp I realised he was talking about putting the sausages on Mum's grave.

I scribbled 'Deedoh' on my notebook and held it out, pointing to him.

He shook his head. 'Rosh-ay,' he said, pointing to himself and the woman. He took my pencil and wrote it down. He spelled it '*Rocher*'. Then he crossed out 'Deedoh' and wrote '*Didot*'.

Mrs Rocher, who was looking very worried now, nudged him again. Mr Rocher noticed this time and frowned and looked like a man who'd said too much.

My mind was racing.

He was saying that someone called Didot had taken sausages to Australia and put them on Mum's grave.

Suddenly I knew who Didot must be.

The bloke with the curly hair, the one I saw in the cafe last night and in our driveway. He must be Didot. The day I saw him at home was the same day I found the sausages.

But why would a bloke fly halfway round the world and risk smuggling sausages into Australia and leave them on a person's grave? Even if they were that person's favourite?

My eyes must have been bulging with the effort of thinking so hard because Mr and Mrs Rocher were looking at me, concerned.

I gave them a smile to show I was OK.

Then I nearly fainted.

Everything fell into place.

Guilt.

That's why a bloke would go all the way to Australia to leave a person's favourite sausages on her grave.

Guilt at knocking her down with his car.

Twelve years after killing her, he was still trying to make himself feel better.

Got you, I thought.

I would have roared it out if I could.

I'm hurrying to the post office now as fast as I can to get Mr Didot's address. It's not that fast because Mr and Mrs Rocher insisted I take the sausages and the bag's really heavy.

Plus I'm feeling a bit of guilt myself. I'm wondering if what I did to Dermot Figgis's car was a bit much given that he didn't even put dog poo on Mum's grave.

No, I've just decided he still deserved it for mocking the memory of a fine woman.

When all this is over, but, I am going to try to learn to control my temper.

First, though, I've got something much more important to do.

I can see the post office up ahead.

Soon I'll know where Mr Didot lives.

And then I can meet that murdering mongrel face to face.

I was just about to go into the post office when I caught a flash of pink out of the corner of my eye.

Across the street, watching me, was the young woman in the pink jeans who'd been staring at me outside the sausage shop.

I waved.

She ducked behind a parked truck.

I dumped the bag of sausages. This was no time to be loaded down with smallgoods. Then I kept on walking.

After a bit, I glanced back. As I thought, she was following me.

I wasn't worried, but. I've been followed heaps of times. There's a kid in my class, Darryn Peck, who used to follow me with his mates and make dumb comments about my throat.

I'm good at getting rid of people who follow me.

I walked casually for a bit, then ducked into a supermarket.

Supermarkets are good for losing people because they always have a back door leading out to the carpark. At least, Australian ones do.

This one didn't.

I stood in a panic, staring at the fruit and veg display where the back entrance should have been.

If the woman in the pink jeans followed me in I was trapped. She was probably a detective who worked with Mr Bernard. The local council probably had her keeping an eye on me, ready to pounce and arrest me if I got too close to exposing Mum's killer.

I was getting very close.

She wouldn't like that.

I thought I could hear her creeping towards me down the cereals and dry goods aisle, handcuffs at the ready.

I didn't dare turn around.

Not more than halfway.

Which was enough to see a plastic swing door between a display of lightbulbs and a freezer cabinet.

I threw myself at the door and burst into a gloomy corridor and sprinted down it to a storeroom full of boxes.

A man's voice shouted at me in French. I saw a patch of daylight and ran for it, knocking over a box of fruit and stubbing my toe on some tins.

I ducked under a half-open roller door, sprinted down a narrow lane, across a road, into a park, wriggled through some thick bushes, came out into a sort of square, crept between some parked cars and found myself standing in front of a building with big windows.

Through the windows I could see shelves of books.

It looked like a public library.

I didn't hesitate.

I went in.

Nothing looks more suspicious than a person gasping for breath outside a public library. They're obviously either on the run or having an anxiety attack because their library books are six months overdue.

Inside I went straight to the shelf furthest from the door and the window, ducked down behind it and grabbed a book.

I pretended to read it.

It was in French of course, but luckily it had lots of pictures so I didn't have to pretend too hard. They were black and white photos. I stared at them in amazement.

For a sec I thought it was a book about the dangers of using too much spray on paddocks. The photos showed areas of land that were totally and completely wrecked. Just mud and dead cows and splintered trees.

It looked even worse than the paddock Paige Parker had sprayed.

Then I spotted something else in one of the photos. There were trenches in the ground with soldiers in them wearing World War One uniforms.

It wasn't sprays that had wrecked the land, it was war.

Someone tapped me on the shoulder.

I spun round and looked up, panicking.

But it wasn't the detective in the pink jeans, it was a plump lady trying to get past with a librarian's trolley.

I jumped up and got out of the way. The woman smiled and pointed to the photo I'd been looking at.

'*Ici*,' she said.

I didn't know what she meant. I hoped that in France librarians aren't allowed to make arrests on behalf of the local council.

Then I realised from her hand-movements that she was saying the photo had been taken nearby. Locally. Something like that.

I thanked her, put the book back and hurried out of the library and round a couple of corners.

She didn't follow me.

I wandered around lost for a while, then found a street I recognised and hurried back to the post office. I had to find Mum's killer before the detective in pink jeans found me.

I looked around carefully as I approched the post office.

No sign of her.

My bag of sausages was still on the footpath. I grabbed a couple for evidence and hurried into the post office.

There was a public phone booth in the corner with a phone book on a string. I went over to it, heart pounding. Somewhere in that book was the address of the man I'd come round the world to find.

I opened it at the Ds, praying there was only one Didot.

A hand grabbed me by the shoulder.

I froze.

Please, I begged silently. Please let it be the librarian with more information about local World War One battles and not the detective in pink jeans.

I turned round.

It wasn't either of them.

The face looking steadily at me with bloodshot eyes had stubble on it and black curly hair on top.

It was Mr Didot.

I was in shock.

Total and complete shock.

That's the only reason I let Mr Didot lead me out of the post office without kicking him and biting him and letting him have it in the privates with whatever stationery I could lay my hands on.

That's the only reason I let him put me into his car.

It was only when we were driving down the street that my brain started working again and I realised what I'd done.

I'd let him kidnap me.

And now he was going to make sure I couldn't tell anyone he'd killed my mum.

Lock me away somewhere.

Or worse.

I felt sick and weak and panicky, but I knew I mustn't give in to the feeling.

I wondered if Mr Didot's car had central locking. If not, perhaps I could fling the door open and dive out.

If only he wasn't driving so fast. Doesn't anyone in France drive slowly? I asked myself gloomily. Not maniac hit-and-run drivers, that's for sure, I replied bitterly.

Then I noticed something very weird.

The way he was looking at me. With a gentle, concerned expression.

Caring.

I've seen psycho-killer movies at friends' houses and psycho killers often pretend to be gentle and concerned and caring but you can always tell they're faking it.

With Mr Didot I couldn't.

His caring expression looked real.

Well, I wasn't going to be sucked in.

I scribbled angrily in my notebook, ripped the page out and held it in front of his face.

'You killed my mother,' it said, 'and I've got the sausages to prove it.'

He stared at the page, frowned and kept on driving.

At least he wasn't looking concerned and caring any more.

Which would make it easier for me when I had him put away for life.

A few minutes later we pulled into the driveway of a house.

I made a mental note of as many details as I could to help Dad find me if I was able get a message to him. The driveway was gravel. The house was two-storey with a slate roof and white shutters. The window-ledges all had flower pots on them. The flowers were all red.

Blood red.

I forced myself to calm down.

If I got hysterical thinking about the danger I was in, I'd never get a confession out of the killer.

I let Mr Didot lead me into the house. He took me through a living-room full of rich-looking old furniture and into an office with used coffee cups and plates all over the desk.

I decided to go for the direct approach. Dad always does and it usually works for him.

'I confess,' I wrote in my notebook. 'I killed her. Signed . . . . . .' I put dotted lines where I wanted Mr Didot's signature to go, tore out the page and handed it to him.

He stared at it with a blank expression, then went over to the desk and switched on a notebook computer.

I couldn't believe what he did next. He typed the confession into the computer. Yes, I thought, heart pounding. The years of guilt have got too much for him. He's going to sign the confession but he doesn't want it to be in my untidy handwriting.

Boy, was I wrong.

Mr Didot didn't print out the confession.

Instead he reached for the mouse button and clicked on a French flag at the top of the screen. Almost instantly my English words on the screen turned into French words. I stared, amazed. It was a computer program that translated from one language to another.

He looked at the confession on the screen, sighed, looked at me and shook his head.

Then he typed some French, clicked an English flag and it turned into English.

'Mr and Mrs Rocher from the sausage shop rang me and told me you'd probably be thinking I killed your mother,' he'd written. 'I didn't. I was in hospital the night she was killed.'

'Prove it,' I typed and clicked the French flag.

'That's why I've brought you here,' typed Mr Didot.

He opened a drawer in the desk and took out a folder. It was full of forms. He let me look at them. They were all in French, but printed on the top of each one was what looked like the name and address of a hospital.

I noticed the same French word on several of the forms.

Rein.

I typed it into the computer and clicked the English flag.

Kidney.

Mr Didot looked uncomfortable. I wondered if it was because the forms didn't prove a thing. He could be a caterer with a contract to supply food to the hospital, including kidneys.

Mr Didot tore the top off one of the forms and gave it to me.

'The hospital will tell you I was a patient that night,' he typed.

While he was typing I noticed that a photo had fallen out of the folder. I picked it up. It showed a younger Mr Didot in a hospital bed connected to a medical-looking machine. The weird thing was, he was wearing a party hat and grinning. The people crowded round the bed looked like they were having a party. Even the machine was wearing a party hat.

Mr Didot saw I had the photo and snatched it from me. He stuffed it back into the folder and shoved the folder back into the drawer.

He seemed anxious I'd seen it.

I was confused.

Was he making the stuff up about the hospital? It didn't look like it.

But I wasn't letting him off that easily.

'If you didn't kill Mum,' I typed, 'why did you go to Australia and leave sausages on her grave?'

Mr Didot looked startled. Then he let out a sigh and typed for a long time.

'I knew your father from when he was here

twelve years ago,' he wrote. 'About a month ago, when he first knew the media were investigating the sprays, he wrote to me.'

I stared at the screen. A month ago? That meant Dad knew the media were sniffing around several weeks before I found out. Why didn't he say anything?

He was hoping the whole thing would blow over, probably.

'I'm an industrial chemist,' typed Mr Didot. 'Your dad asked me to check up on the sprays he was using. It is very hard because the chemical companies do not want to answer my questions. I am spending many nights on the Internet.'

I looked at Mr Didot's bloodshot eyes. Either he was telling the truth or he'd been lying awake worrying like guilty killers do on videos.

'Last week I went to Australia,' typed Mr Didot, 'to talk to the TV people. To tell them they cannot accuse your dad without more proof. They wouldn't listen to me. They wouldn't even let me switch my computer on. I did not want the whole trip to be a waste. So I went to your mother's Australian grave to pay my respects. With her favourite food. It is a custom in my family.'

I've known some pretty good liars in my time. Darryn Peck, for example. He had the whole school fooled when he claimed it wasn't him who let off the starting pistol in assembly.

But he didn't fool me.

I looked hard at Mr Didot. He looked back at me steadily with sad, gentle, concerned, bloodshot eyes.

I wanted him to be lying.

I wanted to have found Mum's killer.

But deep in my guts I wasn't sure. His hands hadn't wobbled guiltily once while he was typing.

I let Mr Didot put me back in the car to drive me to Mr and Mrs Bernard's. I felt sick and numb with disappointment.

As we drove past the sausage shop, Mr Rocher came running out carrying a sort of meatloaf wobbling on a plate.

Mr Didot stopped.

Mr Rocher tried to hand me the plate through the window.

Suddenly I couldn't stand it.

I leaped out of the car, pushed past Mr Rocher and ran. Along streets. Across squares. Down alleyways.

Finally I found Mum's cemetery.

The grass on her grave is soft against my face.

But it's not making me feel better. The longer I lie here, the worse I feel.

It's not fair.

I just wish everyone would stop being so nice to me and tell me who killed my mum.

If you want to find out the truth, play a mouth-organ in a cemetery, that's my advice.

I started playing mine to cheer myself up. And to let Mum know I wasn't beaten.

I can only play part of one tune. Dad taught me 'Waltzing Matilda' on the plane over, but we'd only got halfway through when the flight attendant took the mouth-organ away and locked it up till we'd landed.

I was sitting next to the grave, sadly playing half of 'Waltzing Matilda' for about the sixth time, when a small black dog ran up and sat in front of me. It gazed up, panting happily.

I stopped playing.

The dog jumped up and barked.

It wouldn't stop. I decided to try and distract it so I started playing again.

The dog sat down and listened contentedly.

Despite everything that had happened, I

started grinning. A French dog that liked 'Waltzing Matilda'. Weird. Trouble was, every time I grinned I had to stop playing and every time I stopped playing the dog started barking.

After a while I realised someone was standing behind me, watching.

I stood up.

It was an old bloke, even older than Grandad. He was so frail, his clothes looked like they were propping him up.

He was smiling.

'Her favourite tune,' he said, nodding towards the dog. At least I think that's what he said. 'I play the record for her all the time at home.'

I stared at him.

Not because it's unusual to play records to dogs.

Because he was speaking with his hands.

'You speak sign,' I said. Then I stuffed my hands in my pockets. I hate it when they embarrass me by saying really obvious things.

The old bloke's smile faded. 'When I was very young there was a battle near our house. A banana exploded too close. It blew up my ears.'

Some of his hand-movements were a bit different to the ones I know, but I got the gist. I was pleased to see his ears were still in one piece. On the outside, at least.

I pulled my hands out of my pockets. 'How did you know I speak sign?' I asked.

He frowned at me, thinking.

'Fry them with garlic and onions,' he said.

I realised we had a bit of a language problem. I asked him again, making my hand-movements slow and big.

'Ah, I understand,' he said, making his slow and big too. 'How do I know you speak sign? I know much about you Australian visitors. I watch people's lips. I have been hoping to meet you. I love all Australians.'

Boy, I thought. You obviously haven't met Dermot Figgis or Darryn Peck.

The old bloke's face wrinkled into a scowl and for a sec I thought he had.

Then he said, 'Nobody told me about the party at the cafe last night.' He sighed and gave a shrug. 'Perhaps it's because they know that me and Simone go to bed at seven-thirty.' He patted the dog.

'Why do you like Australians?' I asked.

'Come,' he said. 'I will show you.'

He led me out of the cemetery and across a big paddock. It was a long, slow, muddy walk.

Probably the best long, slow, muddy walk I've been on in my life.

While we walked, the old bloke told me how during World War One the town was attacked by a German sausage. That's what I thought he said. Then I realised he'd said German army.

There were French soldiers defending it, he

went on, and English, but mostly Australian.

Suddenly he stopped.

We were at the other side of the paddock. Running along by the fence was a deep trench, too wide to jump across. I could tell it was old from the weeds and rain gullies in the dirt walls. Parts of it had caved in, but other parts were about twenty times as deep as Erin's sandpit at home.

It would have taken some digging.

For a sec I thought the old bloke was going to tell me the town people dug it in the war to work off the stress of being attacked by the Germans.

He didn't.

'Australians dug that,' he said. 'The Australian soldiers who saved the town.'

He had tears on his cheeks.

I didn't blame him. I'd cry too if Australian soldiers saved my mum and dad.

Then it hit me.

Of course.

That's why everyone here's been so kind to me and Dad. They must treat all Aussies that way. To say thanks for saving their town.

I sat down at the edge of the trench, weak with relief.

Dad didn't do a deal with the local council after all. The reason they look after Mum's grave is gratitude for the war.

The dog was licking my face, probably hoping I'd play 'Waltzing Matilda'.

I was so happy I almost did.

Then I remembered a couple of things and my lips went too stiff to get a note out of the mouth-organ even if I'd wanted to.

One, Mum's killer is still at large.

Two, the old bloke's an expert on Australian visitors.

I looked up at him. My hands were shaking but I got them under control.

'Do you know who killed my mother?' I asked.

The old bloke wiped his eyes on a hanky and looked at me for a long time. At first I didn't think he'd understood me. I pulled Erin's rag doll and plastic car out of my pocket and made a little road in the dirt and crashed the car into the doll and knocked her down.

I hated doing it but I had to be sure he understood.

I did it again.

I only stopped when I couldn't see for tears.

I felt something being pressed into my hand. It was the old bloke's hanky. I wiped my eyes and gave it back to him.

He gestured for me to hand him my notebook. I did.

He wrote something and handed it back.

Even before I made out the words I saw it was a name and address. I jumped up and threw my arms round the old bloke and hugged him.

He looked startled, but I think he liked it.

Thank you, my hug said. Thank you, thank you, thank you for finally telling me the name of the man who killed my mum.

I looked at the name and address.

Boy, was I totally and completely wrong.

It's a woman.

I stood by the trench in a daze, dog dribble drying on my face, staring at my notebook.

My brain felt like stewed apple.

I don't remember saying goodbye to the old bloke and the dog. I was too busy getting used to what he'd just told me.

That the person who killed Mum wasn't the stupid, careless, hairy-knuckle cowboy hoon I'd imagined – it was a woman called Michelle Solange.

That felt very weird.

Michelle has always been one of my favourite names.

I had a pet rat once called Michelle.

Stop it, I told myself. Pull yourself together. Because it doesn't make any difference.

If she's Mum's killer, I'm going to bring her to justice. And if I can lay my hands on a decent quantity of rotting apples, I'm going to teach her car a lesson too.

First I went back to Mum's grave to let her know that everything's under control.

Then I went into town to the tourist map. I found the killer's street. It's on the northern edge of town.

I was about to head over there when I remembered Dad. I'd told him I was going for a walk hours ago.

I imagined him sitting by the window at Mr and Mrs Bernard's, pulling threads out of the carpet and chewing them, which is what he usually does when he gets worried sick.

Suddenly I felt really bad.

I'd been really unfair to Dad, thinking he'd done a deal with the council and losing respect for him like that.

He'd probably wanted to expose Mum's killer but had been scared to in case the locals got angry and yelled at him for lowering the tone of the district. Then he'd have had the Australian embassy yelling at him for lowering the popularity of Aussie tourists in the district.

It must be really scary, having people angry and yelling at you when that's all your father ever did.

Poor Dad, I thought.

I decided not to go straight to the killer's house.

I decided to go to Mr and Mrs Bernard's first and give Dad a hug.

I wish now I hadn't.

At Mr and Mrs Bernard's place the kitchen was empty. I couldn't see Dad anywhere. I hoped he wasn't out leading a search party.

Then I heard voices coming from the lounge-room.

I opened the door and stepped in.

And froze.

Sitting on the settee, next to Mrs Bernard, was the young woman in pink jeans. Next to her was Mr Didot. Opposite them were Mr and Mrs Rocher from the sausage shop.

They were all staring at me.

Every single one of them looked awkward and uncomfortable.

I thought it must have been because they were all detectives and I'd just blown their cover as nice, concerned local citizens. Then I noticed they weren't jumping on me and arresting me to stop me getting at Mum's killer.

I was confused.

I took a step back.

None of them moved.

I had to find out what was going on.

I wish now I hadn't. I wish now I'd run out of the house and gone straight to the killer's place.

Instead I grabbed my notebook and wrote in

big letters 'WHO ARE YOU?' and thrust it at the pink-jeans woman. Mrs Bernard looked at it and translated.

The pink-jeans woman stood up and held her arms out as if she was going to hug me.

I hadn't expected that. I took another step back.

The pink-jeans woman opened her mouth to speak. Mrs Bernard grabbed her arm. She said something to the woman in French. The only word I understood was Dad's name.

The pink-jeans woman gave me a sad, worried look and sat back down.

Mr Didot and Mrs and Mrs Rocher were giving me sad, worried looks too.

I wanted to jump on the coffee table and scream 'WHAT'S GOING ON?'

As it turned out I didn't need to.

Mrs Bernard took my hands in hers and stroked them gently.

'Your father is upstairs,' she said. 'He wants to see you.'

My brain was racing as I went upstairs. Why was everyone looking so sad and worried? Had Dad been offered a recording contract by a French CD company? Had the sausages I'd left outside the post office gone mouldy and someone had eaten them and was suing us?

When Dad opened his door I saw it was much worse than that.

Dad had been crying and he only cries at Disney movies or when things are really, really crook.

'Rowena,' he said, 'I've had some rough news.'

He made me sit on the bed and put his arm round me.

My mind was in a panic.

Was someone sick?

Had someone died?

'Claire rang,' he went on. 'She's had a letter from the TV people. They've come up with some more evidence.'

Dad's voice wobbled as he said evidence, which made my guts wobble too.

'Claire faxed the new evidence to her old science teacher at uni,' continued Dad, 'and he reckons it's kosher.'

I didn't know what kosher was, but Dad's strangled voice was enough to give me a knot in the guts bigger than Western Europe.

'Love,' said Dad, 'it looks like the TV people were right about those sprays. The ones I used before you were born. They probably did what the TV people said they did. They probably stuffed your throat up.'

My brain went to stewed apple again.

Dad started crying again.

I sat there numb, while Dad sobbed, 'I'm sorry, I didn't know,' over and over into my hair.

Then he sat up and wiped his tears and gripped my shoulders and put his face close to mine.

And softly started to sing.

He sang one of my favourite songs, 'I Love You More Than Pickled Onions', and he's never sung it with more emotion in his voice, but I didn't want to hear it.

By the end of the first verse I was feeling sick and dizzy.

I pulled away from Dad and told him I needed to lie down, and left him there and came to my room.

It's not fair.

Dads shouldn't do this to kids.

Tell them this sort of news.

No kid wants to feel angry and let down and violent towards her own dad.

Luckily I don't have to.

Luckily I'm using all my anger up on someone else.

A woman who I'll be going to visit in another hour or so, just as soon as I'm sure everyone in the house is asleep.

A woman who has brought misery and sadness and loneliness and grief into the life of an innocent child.

A woman who deserves to die.

The gun was old.

And heavy.

When I lifted it off the wall of Mr Bernard's workshop, I nearly pulled a muscle.

I didn't care.

It was big.

The barrel was long.

It looked like it could shoot a hole in a fridge. Or a cowardly hit-and-run driver.

Which was exactly what I needed.

It even had a convenient strap for slinging it over your shoulder. I slung it over my shoulder. The wooden part smacked against some hanging cheeses.

I snapped my torch off and held my breath, hoping I hadn't woken anyone up.

It didn't sound as though I had.

Then I saw a dark shape behind the workshop door.

One of the good things about having a dud throat is you can't scream with terror and wake the whole street up.

Inside my head, though, I yelled good and loud.

Then I realised it was just a coat.

A big, old, heavy coat hanging inside the door.

It was as thick as a doormat and I nearly dislocated a shoulder getting it on, and as I walked it dragged on the ground behind me.

But it completely covered the gun. I checked in the hall mirror as I crept out of the house. Only really dumb kids carry big guns along streets at two in the morning without hiding them under coats.

Boy, those World War One soldiers must have had serious muscles to carry those guns.

By the time I'd lugged mine about two kilometres down the road towards the killer's place, I felt like I was carrying a sink.

Even the bullet in the coat pocket was starting to feel heavy. There'd been three in the display case on Mr Bernard's wall. I was glad I'd only brought one.

One was all I'd need.

Then I saw it, up ahead, glowing white in the moonlight behind some dark bushes.

The killer's house.

Her bushes weren't carved into any shapes.

She obviously didn't want to draw attention to herself. I didn't blame her. If I'd killed an innocent member of the public, I wouldn't want to win gardening competitions either.

I checked that the number on the gatepost matched the number in my notebook.

It did.

My guts tightened and suddenly the gun didn't feel so heavy.

I crept past the bushes.

There were no lights on in the house.

I tried the front door. It was locked.

I moved as quietly as I could round to the back. Country people hardly ever lock their back doors, it's a known fact. This place was on the edge of town about half a kilometre from any other houses. I hoped the killer thought it was the country.

She didn't. The back door was locked.

OK, I thought, a window.

I can get through really small windows. Once on Dad's birthday I snuck in through our toilet window with his present. A long-handled toilet brush is almost as big as a rifle.

I moved down the other side of the house looking for an open window.

I wish I hadn't done that.

I really wish I hadn't.

Because that's where it happened.

I found a window. It was only open a bit,

but I was able to get my hand in and release the catch and swing it open.

Peering in, I saw a figure asleep in bed. I could just make out a frilly bed cover. And a frilly dressing gown hanging on the wardrobe door.

My heart was thudding like a battlefield.

I took the bullet from the coat pocket.

I looked at it in the moonlight.

This bullet, I thought, is going to get justice for our family.

When I climb through that window, and wake her up, and point the gun at her, and she sees me loading it with a bullet, she'll know I mean business.

With a bit of luck I won't have to pull the trigger and give away that the gun doesn't actually work and the bullet's just a replica.

With a bit of luck she'll write out a confession so fast she'll need a non-skip ballpoint.

That's what was supposed to happen.

Instead, before I even got one leg through the window, the person in bed rolled over so her sleeping face was in a patch of moonlight.

I stared, my brain spinning.

It was a kid.

A girl of about my age.

She couldn't be the killer. She'd only have been a baby when Mum was killed. She wouldn't even have been driving a pram, let alone a car.

I realised I must be looking at the killer's daughter.

I tried desperately to stop the pictures that were crowding into my head.

Me getting a confession from the girl's mother at gunpoint.

A judge reading the confession and sentencing the mother to life in a maximum security prison with no carpets.

The girl growing up without a mum.

Just like me.

That's when I started trembling.

That's when I knew I couldn't do it.

And that's when I heard the vehicle.

I spun round, peering through the bushes at the headlights coming along the road towards the house.

I prayed it wasn't a police car.

It wasn't, it was an ambulance.

I prayed it would drive past.

It didn't, it stopped at the front of the house.

I ran.

The backyard was like an obstacle course with garden furniture and washing and bean poles and about a million compost heaps.

As I darted between them, the big coat flapped around my legs almost tripping me up and the gun cracked me in the knees.

I didn't dare stop and take them off.

At least when I dived over the back fence the

coat helped cushion my fall onto the mud.

As I picked myself up I heard the ambulance door slam. Mr Bernard must have found the gun missing and panicked. He must have called the ambulance.

He and the other police wouldn't be far behind.

A horrible thought stabbed through me. What if stealing a gun is an even bigger crime in France than running someone over?

It could be me who ends up in the maximum security prison.

I kept on running.

I was in a big ploughed paddock with mud furrows shining in the moonlight.

Then the moon went behind a cloud.

I tripped over and sprawled face-down in the muck.

I didn't care.

Darkness was what I wanted. I picked myself up and staggered on. I felt like a big cockroach in that coat, scuttling through the blackness. Glancing anxiously behind to see if they were following me.

They weren't.

Or if they were, they were doing it with much less panting and falling over and scrambling to their feet and mud-spitting than I was.

Then I tripped for the last time.

Instead of my face hitting cold mud again, I

somersaulted forward into empty air.

And landed so hard on my back that even the coat couldn't stop my brain from scrambling.

When I was able to stand up, I looked around.

Walls twice as tall as me towered up on both sides. I ran my hands over them. They were dirt.

I looked up at the strip of moon-hazed sky overhead and realised where I was.

In an old trench like the one the old bloke showed me.

The perfect place to bury a gun.

I started digging, using the barrel of the gun as a crowbar and the wooden end as a spade.

While I dug I thought bitterly about Mum's killer.

It wasn't over. I wasn't going to let her get away with it. I'd just have to wait till her daughter was old enough to do without a mother.

What age was that?

Twenty? Thirty? Seventy?

Be fair, I told myself, it's not the kid's fault her mother's a criminal.

Just like it's not my fault my father's a ratbag.

She's lucky.

At least her mother only damaged someone else.

At least her mother didn't hurt her.

Not like my father.

Not like Kenny the Cowboy.

Not like the fastest spray gun in the western postal district.

Angry tears flooded my eyes but I kept on stabbing the gun blindly into the dirt.

I had to keep digging to make a hole deep enough to bury the evidence.

Except suddenly it wasn't the gun I wanted to bury, it was the mouth-organ jiggling in my coat pocket.

And the elastic-sided boots Dad bought me last birthday.

And the photo of him in my wallet.

Everything that reminds me of him.

I was crying so hard I wasn't watching what I was doing.

The hole I was digging must have been too close to the wall of the trench.

I was swinging the rifle like a pick axe, eyes squeezed tight against the tears and the sadness and the memory of what a good dad I used to think he was.

Then the trench wall started to collapse.

I felt lumps of dirt cannoning into me and stones stinging my face and before I could jump back a dark object started sliding towards me out of the crumbling wall of the trench.

I put my hands up to protect my head and found myself being pushed backwards by rusty metal.

I tried to stay on my feet but the metal thing

kept coming and wet dirt was showering into my face and my feet slipped on stones and I fell onto my back and the thing came sliding down onto my chest.

I waited to be crushed.

I wasn't.

I'm trapped under it, but.

In the moonlight I can see it's a metal cylinder about the size of the water heater we used to have over the bath. Before Claire and Erin came along and we got one outside.

It's so rusty I can't tell what it is.

It could even be a water heater.

Or one of those big gas cylinders people use if they've got a lot of welding or barbecueing to do.

It could be a million things. Give people a hole and they'll dump anything.

Anyway, I'm lying here, half covered in dirt, trapped under it.

Luckily it's still half in the trench wall, sort of balanced, so it's not actually crushing my chest, just pinning me down. Trouble is, both my arms are buried so I can't even try and shift it. And when I try and wriggle, the thing starts to slip and more bits of trench wall collapse.

I've been here for about half an hour already.

I could be here for days.

I don't care, but.

When your mum's dead and your dad's ruined your life, where else is there to go?

What's that noise?

It sounds like a vehicle bouncing across the paddock. Now it's stuck in the mud. I can hear wheels spinning.

The ambulance?

The police?

I don't know if I want them to find me or not.

Is juvenile remand centre worse than being trapped in a trench under a lump of rusty metal?

Wait on, that voice, calling my name.

It's Mrs Bernard.

Why does her voice do this to me? Make my guts tingle. Make my heart skip. Make me not want to be buried alive.

I'll whistle to attract her attention.

My mouth's too dry. Too much dirt in it.

With my arms buried I can't even clap.

It's not fair.

Normally I can cope with not having a voice, even though it means I can't yell and scream and roar at dopey policemen and rude TV cameramen and grouchy grandparents and suspected killers.

But now I need one.

I'm not asking for much. I don't want to tell long complicated jokes. I don't want to quote Shakespeare. I'm not asking for Mum's gift of the gab. I just want to yell a couple of words.

'I'm here.'

Is that too much to ask, Dad?

Now I'm crying again. Oh well, perhaps if I let the tears run into my mouth I'll be able to whistle.

Hang on.

The mouth-organ.

It's in my coat pocket.

If I can just get one hand free.

The left one's no good, it feels like it's trapped under my bum. The right one's better. I can move it under the dirt. Wriggle it into the pocket.

Got it.

Now, get the mouth-organ up to my mouth without causing another avalanche.

Slowly.

Hope this mouth-organ was specially made for war in the trenches. Hope it's a special model with holes that don't clog up with dirt.

I'll give them a suck just in case.

I don't feel up to the first half of 'Waltzing Matilda'. I'll just blow a note. And again. And again.

I think Mrs Bernard's heard it.

Her voice is getting closer. I can see a torch beam flashing.

There she is, peering over the edge of the trench. She's calling down to me. She's forgotten I don't speak French.

Even when I don't understand a word, her voice makes the hairs on my neck stand up. Or it would do if they weren't caked with mud.

Wait on, she's got people with her.

A row of faces, concerned and anxious, staring down at me.

Mr Didot.

Mrs and Mrs Rocher from the sausage shop.

The woman in pink jeans.

Jeez, I've never seen a group of nice people so desperate to help people with bits missing. Even if they're detectives, they're incredibly dedicated. It's 3 a.m. It's starting to rain. And now they're climbing down into the trench.

Please, go easy. If you start a mud slide, we're all history.

They've made it.

Mrs Bernard didn't stop talking all the way down, but at least she switched to English.

'I blame myself, Rowena,' she said. 'I should

have guessed you'd find out who the driver was.'

I wish I could tell her not to be so hard on herself. But I'm still groping in my pocket with my free hand for my notebook.

Mrs Rocher is unwrapping something and holding it out to me.

It's a slice of something with bits in it.

Mr Rocher is reading from an English phrase book.

'Bolled ship's had yelly.'

I think he means boiled sheep's head jelly.

I wish I hadn't worked that out.

Mr Rocher has just dropped the phrase book. He's staring at the metal thing I'm lying under. He's looking horrified. He's yelling at Mrs Bernard. Perhaps it's a bit of his old fridge and he's just remembered he left some duck nostrils in it.

They're all staring at it.

They all look horrifed.

They're all talking to me in French.

I can tell from their hand-movements they don't want me to move. Not even a tiny bit. I think Mr Rocher would prefer it if I didn't even breathe.

The woman in pink jeans is making a frantic call on her mobile phone.

'Be brave, little Ro,' Mrs Bernard is saying. 'Help will be here soon.'

The danger of a mud slide must be even worse than I can see from here.

Mr Didot has got his notebook computer with him. He's switching it on. He's crouching down next to me. He wants me to read the screen.

'Your dad's going to be OK,' it says. 'I've had a reply from the top agricultural chemical lab in Sweden. They checked the amounts of spray your dad was told to use. The amounts were too high. He was told to use too much. It wasn't his fault.'

I'm struggling to digest this.

I think it means that the salesman who sold Dad the spray lied to him about how much he should use.

I think it means that.

I'm finding it a bit hard to concentrate because I'm also watching Mrs Bernard and Mr Rocher's hand-movements and I've just realised why they're whispering so frantically to each other.

The big rusty metal thing I'm lying under.

It's a bomb.

Isn't it amazing how a few seconds can change your life totally and completely for ever?

A bomb can explode.

A car can hit you.

Somebody can tell you something.

And from then on you're never the same.

I'll never be the same, not after what Mrs Bernard has just told me.

I thought what she told me about the bomb was mind-boggling enough.

'It's not a bomb,' she said, stroking my cheek. 'It's a shell.'

'What's the difference?' I typed one-handed on Mr Didot's computer that he was kindly holding for me.

'A bomb comes from a plane,' she said. 'A shell comes from a cannon.'

I could tell there was more.

Mrs Bernard took a deep breath.

'This shell is from World War One,' she continued. 'It is more than eighty years old. It is very fragile. One tiny movement and boom. You must be very still.'

I wished desperately she hadn't used the word boom.

It's really hard to be very still when your whole body's shaking.

I typed on the computer with the tiniest finger movements I could.

'Get out. Get to safety.'

Then, because if they did get out this would be my last chance to write anything, I also typed, 'If I die please bury me with my mum.'

I needn't have bothered.

They didn't get out to safety.

They stayed where they were, looking at me with such care and concern.

I didn't understand.

'Rowena,' said Mrs Bernard softly, 'you are with your mother here.'

I understood that even less.

'She is in all of us,' Mrs Bernard went on.

I thought I understood that. I thought she meant they remembered Mum fondly. I thought they were being sweet and kind and religious.

Boy, was I wrong.

I saw Mrs Bernard exchange glances with the others. Mr Rocher gave a small nod.

Mrs Bernard turned back to me.

'Your mother did a wonderful, generous thing,' said Mrs Bernard. 'Years before she was killed, she instructed that when she died, parts of her body could be given to people who needed them.'

Mrs Bernard pointed to the small group standing around her.

'We are the people who needed them,' she said.

I looked at her, trying to understand.

'Twelve years ago Mr Rocher was almost dead from a heart disease,' said Mrs Bernard gently. 'His heart was finished. Then he was given your mother's heart.'

Mr Rocher gave me a small nod. I'd never seen so much love in the eyes of a bloke I wasn't related to.

Although, my spinning brain tried to tell me, in a way I was.

I wasn't listening to it.

Mrs Bernard was speaking again.

'Edith was blind,' she said, pointing to the woman in pink jeans. 'Then she was given your mother's eyes.'

I stared at Edith.

She stared back at me, her eyes shining in the moonlight.

Except they weren't her eyes.

'Mr Didot,' continued Mrs Bernard, 'was on a kidney machine. Then he was given your mother's kidneys.'

Mr Didot held up his computer.

'Thank you,' said the screen.

I didn't type 'you're welcome'. I was thinking of the party hats in the hospital.

I felt a stab of pain in my chest and it wasn't just the big lump of high explosive pressing on it.

'And I . . .' said Mrs Bernard. She stopped. Her eyes were full of tears. For a second she couldn't speak. Then she did.

'I had an accident,' she said. 'A child was drowning. I dived into the river. There was wire. My throat was damaged. Then I was given your mother's voice.'

For the first time I noticed the small scar on her neck.

I stared at her, numb, for what could have been hours.

At some point she reached out and stroked my face. 'I was lucky,' she said sadly. 'My condition wasn't as serious as yours. The operation was a big risk. Most fail. Mine was a success.'

Suddenly feelings started swirling through my whole body.

I wanted to kill them all.

If you'd told me this morning that I'd want to kill people with bits of my mother in them, I wouldn't have believed you.

But I did.

All I had to do was give the shell a thump.

I probably didn't even have to do that.

My heart was probably thumping enough as it was.

Then there was a yell from above us.

'Hang on, Tonto.'

A figure was tumbling down into the trench in a spray of dirt.

Dad.

'Don't panic,' he yelled. 'I've got it.'

Before anyone could move, he grabbed the shell and tried to wrestle it off me.

Everyone panicked.

Mrs Bernard yelled in French.

I yelled in one-handed English.

Dad wasn't listening. He flung himself down next to me and wriggled into the dirt and tried to push the shell off me. He wasn't very successful. The shell slipped further out of the trench wall, onto us both.

Mrs Bernard and the others put their arms over their faces.

The shell didn't explode.

I saw the veins next to Dad's ears bulging. He was supporting the weight of the shell, stopping it from crushing us.

It wasn't a good time to say what I said next, but I couldn't stop myself.

'Why didn't you tell me?' I yelled at him tearfully with my free hand. It was flying about so furiously it almost bashed the shell.

'Why didn't you tell me about Mum's bits?'

Dad took a deep breath.

He was silent for a while. I started to think he couldn't speak because of the weight of the shell.

He looked sadly at Mrs Bernard and the others. Then he looked back at me and sighed.

'I was ashamed,' he said quietly. 'Ashamed I hadn't saved all of her for you.'

My heart stopped.

Did he mean . . .?

He couldn't. When Mum died I was a small baby. Her throat bits would have been about eight sizes too big for me.

'Mum wanted to give her body to help others,' Dad was saying. 'It was her wish. My wish was you'd think Mum was buried in Australia where you could feel close to her. All of her. For ever.'

I understood.

I shut my eyes.

I remembered how close to her I'd always felt, sitting by her grave in Australia.

My insides went warm, just thinking about it.

Then I realised Dad was still speaking.

'There's another reason I didn't tell you the truth about Mum,' he was saying. 'I . . . I didn't want you to know it was my fault she was killed.'

I turned my head towards Dad in the dirt.

His face was very close to mine.

I stared at him.

He took another deep painful breath. Even though Mrs Bernard's torch was getting a bit dim, I could see the tears in Dad's eyes.

'Mum brought me here to see my grandfather's grave,' he went on, 'so I could understand why my dad's such a ratbag. Him growing up without a dad and all. If Mum hadn't been trying to help my dud family, she wouldn't have been in France and she wouldn't have been killed.'

Over the years I've seen a lot of pain on Dad's face, specially when I catch him watching me when he thinks I'm not looking, but I've never seen as much pain as I saw at that moment.

I felt a stab in my chest. For a sec I thought the shell was slipping more. Then I realised it was a sob.

I knew how he felt.

All those years I'd thought Mum's death had something to do with me being born.

All those years me and Dad had been feeling the same thing and we hadn't known it because we hadn't told each other our side of the story.

'Such a waste,' Dad was saying. 'Her lovely, lovely life wasted and it was my fault.'

I reached out my free hand and put it on his cheek.

Then I took it off so I could tell him.

'Mum's death wasn't your fault,' I said, moving my hand gently in front of his straining, tear-streaked face. 'And it wasn't a waste.'

I looked up at Mrs Bernard, Mr and Mrs Rocher, Mr Didot and Edith, who were peering down at me, faces soft with care and concern.

'That's not a waste,' I said, pointing to them.

I was shocked I'd said it.

But I meant it.

Before I could get my breathing under control, I had another thought.

What Mum wanted could still happen.

Dad could still visit his grandfather's grave. He could still have a chance to understand his dad's side of the story.

If we could get out from under this shell, Mum's mission could still be successful. It wouldn't have ended in vain.

As I turned to Dad to tell him this, I had an incredible feeling.

I was carrying on Mum's mission.

Which means I've got a part of Mum in me too.

Dad was struggling again with the shell.

'Get off her, you mongrel,' he grunted, veins bulging.

I felt the weight lift from my chest and suddenly I was being dragged out from under the rough metal.

Mrs Bernard pulled me to my feet and

wrapped her arms round me and shielded me with her body.

Well, the bits of it that are hers.

Dad groaned and the shell dropped back onto his chest.

The others put their arms over their faces again.

The shell didn't explode.

'Get her somewhere safe,' said Dad. 'Now.'

Before I could get my arms free to talk to him, Mrs Bernard started moving me away down the trench.

Dad looked at me as I went. 'I was wrong,' he said. 'I should have told you the truth about Mum. I stuffed it up.'

I wriggled round in Mrs Bernard's arms to face Dad. I still couldn't get my hands free to reply. In the torchlight I noticed something gleaming in the dirt near his head.

My guts gave a lurch.

It was a skull.

The skull of an old soldier.

It could even be the skull of Dad's grandfather.

Dad saw it. He stared at it sadly.

Then the shell started slipping further out of the trench wall. I wanted to throw myself back under it and stop him being crushed, but Mrs Bernard held me tight.

Dad shifted his body and managed to stop it.

'I know what you're thinking,' he said through clenched teeth. 'I've stuffed everything else up, I'm probably gunna stuff this up as well.'

As Mrs Bernard pulled me away along the trench, my eyes were so full of tears I couldn't see if Dad was speaking to me or the skull.

Why's it taking them so long?

With the amount of gear they've got here, you'd think they'd have him out by now.

If I was the French version of the State Emergency Service and I had cranes and scaffolding and generators and lights and an army of bomb-disposal experts in padded suits, I'd have had Dad out of there hours ago.

OK, I know the shell's so fragile that the slightest bump could blow him and them into the next country.

And I know the edge of the trench is so crumbly that they have to reinforce it before they can get the crane close enough.

And I know the shell's slipped so far out that they daren't try and get scaffolding in next to Dad in case the whole thing comes down on them.

But I still reckon I'd have him out by now.

And then I could get home to bed instead of hanging around behind this security tape having painful thoughts.

Like how, even though I really want to blame Dad for what he did to me with the spray, I'm having trouble doing it.

Because if I had a dad like Dad's, a dad who was always angry and yelling at me and never showed he loved me, I'd probably get sucked in by a friendly, caring, older chemical salesman too.

A salesman who seemed to like me.

A salesman who took me under his wing.

A salesman who wanted to teach me things.

I probably wouldn't notice he was doing all that just to sell me more chemicals either.

I'd probably trust the scumbag just like Dad did.

This is ridiculous.

What are they doing over there?

I've built really complex Lego rescue operations in less time than they're taking over there.

If I climb onto the roof of this four-wheel drive, I can just see Dad down in the trench.

Oh no, the shell's slipped out even more.

Dad's having to support most of the weight of it.

I can see his arms trembling with the effort.

He's giving it everything he's got, but how much longer can he take the weight?

If I was the French version of the State Emergency Service I'd be feeding him onion soup to keep his strength up. And I wouldn't have that ambulance parked where he can see it and get depressed.

Thank God Dad's used to giving things everything he's got.

Like when he first married Mum and started the farm and everyone told him it wouldn't work.

Including the bank, the stock and station agent and his dad.

He showed them, but.

'Every day,' he told me once, 'I'd look at Mum's tummy getting bigger with you, then I'd go out into the paddocks and give it everything I'd got.'

Now I'm crying.

I don't want to because if Mrs Bernard sees me she's liable to get all motherly and take me home.

Oh come on, you blokes, work faster.

He can't last much longer.

He's my dad and I want you to get him out.

I'm yelling encouragement to him, but he can't see my hands from down there.

If only Mum was here to yell with her voice.

Wait a sec, I've had an idea.

Mrs Bernard was brilliant.

For a woman who's never sung in public before, she was amazing.

OK, she got to read the words off my notepad, but she also did a great job with the tune and she's only heard Mum's song a few times and most of those were twelve years ago.

I couldn't even play her the cassette because it's back at the house and I was worried Dad wouldn't hold out that long.

Mrs Bernard's guts must have been in a knot as we walked to the edge of the trench. I know mine were. For a start we weren't even meant to have climbed over the security tape.

When the rescue workers saw us, I was sure they'd make us go back.

They started yelling and pointing, but we just ignored them and started singing.

Mrs Bernard really belted it out and Dad

looked up almost straight away. He frowned at first, then gave the sort of crooked grin people do while they're holding up huge weights.

I made my hand-movements as big as I could so he'd know I was singing too.

Then I heard other voices joining in behind us.

I turned round.

Mr Didot and Edith and Mr and Mrs Rocher had followed us. They were singing as well, peering over Mrs Bernard's shoulder to see the words.

They couldn't pronounce half of them and they were even more out of tune than Dad usually is.

It didn't matter.

By the time we'd got to the chorus bit –

'*I know you love me*
I know you're doing your best,
That's why I'm not angry
You've got my head in an ants' nest.'

– Dad's legs had stopped trembling and his shoulders had straightened up.

Which was just as well because suddenly my shoulders were shaking with sobs.

It was Mrs Bernard's singing that did it.

Even though Mum has been dead twelve years, her voice was still alive.

Helping me save Dad.

And her heart.

And her eyes.

And her kidneys.

I looked up at the singing faces gazing down at me and I knew I was being given the one thing I've always wanted more than Mum's voice.

Her love.

At that moment one of the rescue workers trying to get a nylon crane sling in position slipped and bumped the shell.

The shell slid out further.

Other rescue workers yelled in alarm.

Dad was only just able to hold it. I don't reckon he would have if we hadn't been singing.

Then suddenly the crane sling was in position.

The rescue workers started yelling again, instructions this time.

The crane motor revved, the cable tightened, and slowly, slowly, slowly the shell was lifted off Dad.

He was free.

Bomb disposal experts dragged him up out of the trench.

He was surrounded by people slapping him on the back and kissing him on both cheeks.

I couldn't even get to him.

The truth is, I held back.

I wanted to hug him, but something was stopping me.

What if I put my arms round him and it didn't feel right?

What if even though my brain knew it wasn't his fault about the spray, my guts wouldn't let me forgive him?

What then?

I didn't get a chance to think of an answer.

Suddenly the crowd around Dad fell back.

A woman was walking slowly towards him across the rescue site. She was wearing an ambulance driver's uniform.

The local people all stared at her, and then at Dad, and nudged the non-local rescue workers and told them to shut up.

I felt arms slip round me and hold me tight.

It was Mrs Bernard.

The woman stopped in front of Dad and looked him in the face.

In the bright rescue lights I saw her cheeks were wet with tears.

Mrs Bernard stepped closer to Dad and took me with her.

The woman said something to Dad in French. Mrs Bernard translated.

'My name is Michelle Solange.'

Suddenly I had a knot in my guts the size of Australia, including Tasmania.

The woman spoke again. Mrs Bernard hesitated, then translated.

'I killed your wife.'

Some of the onlookers gasped.

I did inside.

Dad blinked.

Still the woman kept looking straight at him.

'My baby daughter was very sick,' she continued. 'I was rushing her to the hospital. I was in a panic. That's why when I hit your wife I did not stop.'

For the first time she looked at the ground.

'Also,' she said quietly, 'I was scared they would take me away from my daughter.'

She looked at Dad again.

Dad still had no expression on his mud-streaked face, but I could see his eyes were red and I knew it wasn't just because of the time being 4.20 a.m.

'To try to make amends,' said the woman, 'I became an ambulance driver. I have helped save hundreds of road victims. But it is not enough. So I have come to you to say what I should have said twelve years ago.'

Mrs Bernard paused, and I realised it was because her throat was choked with tears.

Finally she whispered the woman's last words.

'I'm sorry.'

There was a long silence. Dad and the woman looked at each other.

Then Dad did a wonderful thing.

He lifted his arms and put them round the woman and held her to him.

I looked at them, two weeping parents who'd both just tried to do their best.

And I knew in my guts I wanted to hug him too.

I did most of my crying at Mum's grave.

Mrs Bernard and Mr Didot and Mr and Mrs Rocher and Edith did a fair bit too, specially when I laid the sausages next to Mum's headstone.

But we did some laughing as well.

And some singing and mouth-organ playing.

Mum would have liked that.

Dad did most of his crying at his grandfather's war grave. He's still doing some now.

I don't blame him.

Standing here among the hundreds of white stone crosses, it's hard not to shed a tear.

A lot of these young Aussie blokes were dads when they were killed in the war. Dads who were just doing their best.

A lot of kids had to grow up without them.

That chemical salesman might even have been one.

I reckon that's pretty sad.

Specially for someone like me who's growing up with one of the world's top dads.

Just now me and Dad had one of the best hugs we've ever had and Dad told me he's planning to do two things when we get back to Australia.

First he's going to put a metal plaque on our biggest apple tree in memory of his grandfather.

Then he's going to go and make his dad a bacon and jam sandwich.

I reckon Mum'll be pretty happy to see that.

She won't be there in person, of course, but I will, so that's almost the same.

And then afterwards I'm going to use my gift of the gab to tell Paige Parker everything that's happened.

And when I do I'll make sure I give this place a special mention.

Because if the TV people want to broadcast the truth about Dad and the sprays and me, they should tell the whole story.

It's only fair.

The Other Facts of Life

by Morris Gleitzman

Ben is behaving very strangely.

He's been shutting himself in the bathroom every day for two weeks. His parents are worried. Is it time they told him about THE FACTS OF LIFE?

But Ben actually has some other questions he needs to ask. Whatever it takes, he's determined to get some answers. And so begins a crusade that's both deadly serious – and very, very funny.

Second Childhood

by Morris Gleitzman

Mark's father has always wanted him to be a Somebody. But unless Mark picks up at school, it looks like he's heading down the wrong track. Until . . . Mark and his friends discover they've lived before. Not only that – they were Famous and Important People!

But then they find out they've been responsible for several of the world's big problems. So Henry Ford, Queen Victoria, Albert Einstein and even a famous racehorse get together to see if they can make up for their terrible mistakes . . .